LAST HOPE

EMMANUELLE

USA TODAY BESTSELLING AUTHOR

SNOW

Smart Lily
Publishing

VE
HOPE

CARTER HILLS BAND UNIVERSE
(SUGGESTED READING ORDER)

Carter Hills Band series
False Promises

HEART SONG DUET
Blindsided
Forevermore

Whiskey Melody series
Sweet Agony

SECOND TEAR DUET
Cruel Destiny
Beautiful Salvation

BREATHLESS DUET
Wild Encounter
Brittle Scars

Upon A Star series
Last Hope

Midnight Sparks

Love Song For Two series
<u>Lonesome Heart Duet</u>
Fallen Legend
Rising Star

<u>Two of Us Duet</u>
Snowbound

Wicked Love

All titles available at
emmanuellesnow.com

For the best experience, read in the order as shown above

TRIGGER WARNINGS

Disclaimer

My books are realistic and emotional love stories.

I'm an advocate for mental health, and some topics could be sensitive for certain readers since they are portrayed as close to real life as possible.

I've listed the potential trigger warnings for each title on my website.

Be advised that those trigger warnings could potentially be spoiler alerts for the storylines.

Those sensitive topics have been written with the utmost care and respect. Please reach out if you have questions or comments.

All books contain sexuality, mature content, and language not intended for people under 18 years of age.
For other readers' sake, please avoid spoilers in your reviews.

Thank you and have a wonderful day!

Emmanuelle

emmanuellesnow.com

To my husband,
Because there's no one else like you.
Together, we always achieve greatness.
And you keep me safe.
I love you.

To Shalini
Even when darkness creeps in,
there is always hope for better days.

BECOME A VIP
TO NEVER MISS A THING

Snow's VIP

Join **Emmanuelle Snow's VIP newsletter** for all the cool stuff, promos, new releases, giveaways, and gifts.

emmanuellesnow.com

Snow's Soulmates

Join Emmanuelle Snow's Facebook VIP group, **Snow's Soulmates**, to chat with her and other readers, get updates, and more bonus content.

facebook.com/groups/snowvip

*"You never know how strong you are
until being strong is the only choice you have."*
– unknown

OUR LOVE STORY
THE SONG

Ooooh, you caught my eyes that
    night
Wearing a dress that made you look
    divine
Soon (too soon) you vanished into
    the night
And I searched for you every day for
    months
I believed for a while you were a
    fragment of my imagination
A woman I'd created from my
    deepest dreams
A woman I'd created from my heart
    earnest wishes

[CHORUS]

I never imagined you'd walk back
    into my life

One year was way too long not to
    have you by my side
I never imagined you'd be on my
    front porch that night
Asking for nothing, but giving
    everything
One year was way too long not to
    have you by my side
Now that you're here, I'm holding
    on to you till the end of time
Now that you're here, I'm telling
    you I want you to be mine

Ooooh, you caught my eyes with
    only a smile
Making me a better man just with a
    sight
I could feel you in the night, when I
    lay alone in the dark
And I wished for you in my dreams
    for months
I believed, for a moment, I made
    you up
A love I'd never known was possible
A love I'd never known could be so
    strong

[CHORUS]
Ooooh, now that you're here, I'm
    holding on to you
Loving you with every fiber of my
    heart
This thing we share is stronger than
    any word could express

I know deep inside we were meant
    to be from that first night
That you and I were what love at
    first sight is all about
A story worthy only of fairy tales
The princess and the knight
The ones that you wished for when
    you were little
(When you were a little girl)
The ones that gave you hope to fight
    and survive
(I'll forever be thankful you came to
    me that night)
The ones love songs are made of
(Now you get to sing your own)
The ones that'll travel through time
(Because everyone deserves to
    believe in happy endings)

[CHORUS]
Love, my heart wouldn't be full
    without you
Love, you are my dreams come true
Love, I'll love you with everything
    that I am

Ooooh, I love
Ooooh, I love you forever

Music and lyrics by Carter Hills and Riley Burns

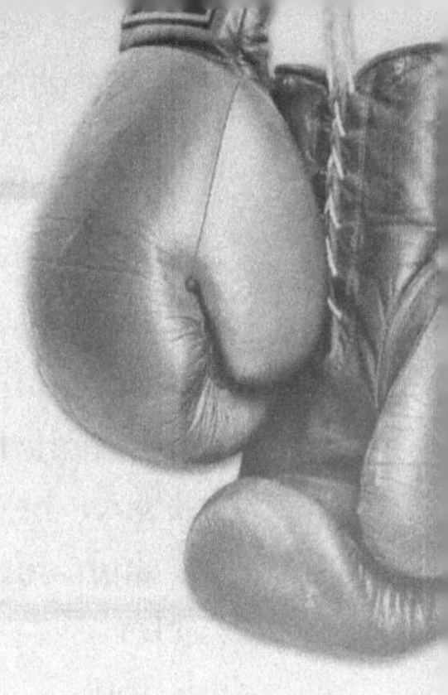

Chapter 1

Riley

Our eyes met. Something passed between us. Attraction. Recognition. Yearning. Maybe a mix of all three. And much more. I brought the tumbler to my lips, relishing the burning sensation of the whiskey as it slid down my throat.

A gear shifted inside me.

My heart did one of its moves. The one where it got all bothered and excited.

I fastened my grip around the glass in my hand.

The woman pushed her long, curled blonde hair over one shoulder, giving me a perfect view of her lickable, slim neck. *Lickable?* Was that even a word? I pushed the thought away. I was a man on a mission.

The vampiric side of me—the one I hadn't known existed until now—emerged in full force.

I blinked.

The temptation to bite the soft flesh of her neck multiplied by the second.

The woman smiled, and all my restraints broke loose. They caught fire and burned to ashes in the dark night.

I gave her a subtle nod as I continued staring, hoping for a slight hint of encouragement from her.

Her red-painted lips pursed as she mouthed *Hey* in my direction.

Smoothing my palm over my trousers, I made a beeline for her, my steps light and focused, not allowing the sea of people to break our eye contact. The air around us heated up. We were outdoors, but it felt as if someone had cranked up the thermostat. Slowly, I raked my fingers through my brown hair, gelled to perfection tonight, doing my best not to mess it up. From an outsider's point of view, I bet I looked in control—the opposite of how I really felt. No one in the business needed to know how unruly my heart was behaving. Or the tremble that had started in my fingers. The flickers of excitement that burned in my core.

A server passed by, and I discarded my tumbler before grabbing two champagne flutes from his tray.

In two long strides, I reached the woman in the red lace dress. Her smile reached her eyes when I offered her the sparkling alcohol. "To a great night and even greater company," I said as we clinked our glasses. "I'm Riley." I held out my hand for her to shake. Our palms met, and a jolt of heat surged through me, setting my insides ablaze in a way no woman ever had. Her touch alone threatened to make me combust.

"I'm Devon."

I lifted our joined hands to my lips and kissed the back of hers.

Her soft chuckle resonated through me. "I can already tell you're a gentleman."

"My mama taught me well. So, what brings you here, Devon? I've never seen you at one of these country music parties before."

"Oh, you go to these a lot? This is my first time. It's quite intimidating. A friend of mine invited me, but she's running late."

I followed her gaze across the rooftop bar. Country music singers, songwriters, and musicians counted for more than half of the patrons here, and together, they'd won enough awards to fill an entire room. Woven through them were music producers, managers, movie stars, and their dates. Yeah, to someone unfamiliar, the crowd could easily appear impressive.

My man, Carter Hills, waved at me when my eyes drifted to him. I raised my glass in his direction. He was not only one of the biggest artists here tonight, but also one of my protégés and closest friends. Over the years, we rose to the top of this industry together, our friendship growing stronger with each album. We had each other's backs. Always.

"All these people, they aren't as intimidating as they look once you get to know them. Most of them are pretty great actually. Down to earth, and genuinely nice. Don't let their success make you nervous. Looking great is part of their job description. But there's much more to them. Well, to some of them at least."

The woman snickered and clutched my elbow, balancing her weight on her four-inch nude stilettos. "You seem like the kind of man who knows a lot about the country music scene, am I right?"

I took another sip of my drink and shrugged, my eyes trained on her face, enjoying the tilt of her red lips. "You could say that. I've been around these folks my entire life, but an active part of their world for almost a decade."

Devon's gray-blue eyes flared. "You're a country singer? Ohmygod, I'm sorry if I didn't recognize you." A flush crept along her neck and cheeks. The same neck I was still dying to feast on.

"Nah. I'm not. Believe me, you don't want to hear me sing. It may burst your eardrums. No kidding."

She grinned at me, and my heart swelled in my chest. "Who are you then? What's your superpower?"

"I'm a manager." I pointed to Carter, now deep in a conversation with Rita L. Sterling, a music producer. "I manage this fellow's career, amongst others."

Devon moved closer and lowered her voice to a whisper as if she feared someone would hear her. Not a chance with the chatter and music surrounding us. "Is that Carter Hills? I'm sorry. I'm not a groupie, I swear, but I thought I recognized him earlier when I walked in."

"Yeah, that's him. I can introduce you later."

She shook her head, the blush on her cheeks darkening. "No, you don't have to. I-I'm nobody here. I'm not part of this world. This night is surreal, I—"

A waitress bumped into my side and lost her footing, sending an entire tray of red wine glasses crashing all over me.

Time seemed to slow. I blinked as my clothes absorbed every drop.

"Oh, shit. I'm…I'm so sorry. It's…oh gosh, it's my first night here. I'm so, so sorry. I-I messed up. Wh-what can I do?" she asked, her eyes glistening with tears as she righted the now-empty wine glasses on the splattered tray. "Ohmygod. I ruined your shirt, sir. This is…this is so unprofessional. I'll get fired over this. Wait here, I-I'll be right back. I will…I'll get my purse. Dry-cleaning is on me."

I wrapped my hand around her wrist before she could run away and leveled my eyes with hers. "Stop. Breathe.

It's just a shirt. I own a dozen more just like it. You won't get fired because nobody will say anything to your boss. I might even have been the one who bumped into you. I should've stood on the side of the deck. See? I'm standing in the way."

The waitress raised her watery eyes, studying me as if there was a *but* about to come out of my lips. There wasn't.

"What's your name?"

"Daph…Daphne."

"Well, Daphne. Breathe in. Breathe out. It'll help to calm your nerves."

She filled her lungs with a deep inhale.

"Yeah, like this." Her shoulders dropped. "See? Much better. Listen, now you go back there," I pointed to the bar, "fill this tray up, smile, and get on with your night. Don't let this little incident affect you. You're doing a great job."

She blinked and swallowed hard, a quiver of a smile trembling over her lips. "How-how can you tell? You don't even know me, sir."

"It doesn't matter. I'd recognize a hard worker anywhere. I have a flair for finding good people. It's my superpower." I fished a business card out of the inner pocket of my now damp jacket. "If waitressing doesn't work out or you're ever looking out for a job, gimme a call. I might be able to put in a good word for you. Don't worry. The sun always comes out after the storm."

"Wow…huh…thank you. I… This… That's the nicest thing someone has ever said to me." She clutched my business card, pressed it against her chest as if I'd just promised her the world. With a shy smile, she turned and walked away, chin raised and back straight.

Warmth filled me. Daphne would be okay. She just needed a pep talk. And I happened to be good at those too.

Perhaps I possessed more than just one superpower after all.

Devon leaned closer, and her eyes widened in stunned disbelief. Her perfume wrapped around me, tipping my senses into a dizzy haze. She smelled like spring and rain. Fresh and flowery. I burned the fragrance to my memory. Even my heart seemed to enjoy it as it expanded in my chest and drummed faster.

"Wow. That was… That was amazing. Most people would have screamed at the poor girl or threatened to get her fired. Instead, you boosted her self-confidence. That's very noble of you. You are a good man, Riley."

I looked down and pinched the fabric of my stained shirt to unglue it from my chest. "Thank you. It was just a clumsy mishap. Now, would you excuse me for a minute? I need to freshen up." I grimaced as she grinned at me, the gleam in her eyes captivating me.

Her smile grew wider, and she gave a gentle nod. "Go ahead. I can't wait to see how you manage to come back still dressed in these clothes. This should be interesting." She wrinkled her nose at my drenched state and said, "Yeah, very interesting."

I smiled. Like a fool. There was no way I could hold it back. Falling under this woman's charm felt like breathing. Easy. Natural. And imperative. "Wait and see. I may surprise you. I always find ways to turn impossible situations around."

Devon chuckled. "I'm sure you do. While you are in there cleaning up, I'll order us more drinks. Whiskey?"

"On the rocks," I said, holding back a grin. Did Devon notice what I was drinking earlier? If so, it made her even more attractive. I dreaded walking away from her, not ready to escape the magnetism that had settled between us. "I'll be quick."

We eye-fucked each other for a few seconds, my pulse spiking at the way her eyes brought her whole face to life.

Full lashes, high cheekbones, straight nose, heart-shaped lips. She was every shade of beautiful. With just one glance in my direction, this woman had captured my heart the moment I first saw her. It made no sense, but I wasn't about to overthink it.

So far, our encounter was the highlight of my night—of my day, maybe even my week.

With a sigh, I broke eye contact.

In a hurry to get back to her, I weaved through the bar crowd, my jacket now open, my soaked shirt sticking to my abs, and the front of my trousers molded to my thighs. Nothing about being wet and dressed up felt good. I was pretty sure even my socks were damp. I frowned at my predicament, wondering how I was supposed to get through the night in clothes soaked with red wine. It wasn't as if I had a change of clothes in my car or something. It wasn't as if I could just run home and change, even though I lived less than ten miles away. Tonight, I had no intention of letting Devon out of my sight, even for just a few minutes.

In the men's room, I peeled off my once-white shirt, gave it a disapproving look, and dropped it in the trash. A complete loss. I couldn't save it even if my life depended on it. After dabbing my trousers with paper towels, I turned the undershirt around and tucked it into my pants. I used more paper towels to soak up the excess wine from my jacket and put it back on. The look wasn't perfect, but in the dark bar, nobody would look too closely to notice.

I eyed myself in the mirror one last time, fixed my hair and the lapel of my jacket, and with determination in each step, made my way back into the night, looking for the woman in the red dress.

Chapter 2
Devon

"Nicole, where are you?" I asked myself in a whisper, a frown pinching my brows. I looked around for the umpteenth time, hoping to catch a sight of her in the crowd. Surrounded by strangers, I suddenly wished we'd come together. I wanted to leave, but since these were the moments of freedom I'd been longing for, I stayed and decided to give her another thirty minutes.

People here dressed in gorgeous dresses and fitting suits. My gaze wandered around the rooftop, taking in the sights, until it landed on him. In that instant, I forgot all about Nicole being late. I forgot this party, the hum of the conversation that surrounded me, the glass I was holding. I even forgot to breathe. Silence permeated me, and all I could hear was the pounding of blood rushing through my veins and my heart thudding against my ribs.

Just a few yards away, I had a clear view of the man. There was a casual elegance about him. His suit fitted as if it had been tailored for him. Dark brown hair, bright eyes, a square jaw with a hint of stubble, he was my idea of perfection. How could I look anywhere else?

Energy radiated from him and swirled around me. It ignited every one of my cells. Something about him appealed to my entire being. Nothing rational. But a fascination, a connection. It was there. As if my soul recognized him.

My eyes zoomed in on the smile grazing his lips as he listened to people talking to him or gestured with his glass of whiskey.

The world ceased to exist for me. The only sound that reached me was the loud thumping of my heart resonating through my skull. Not from fear. But lust. And something so powerful, it weakened my knees.

My mouth went dry, and I raised my drink to my lips, savoring the last drops as they eased the aridness in my throat. Fidgeting with the gold chain around my wrist to avoid fanning myself, a tug-of-war stirred inside me. Should I or shouldn't I?

If I went to the man, would he acknowledge me? Would it seem gauche to approach him first? Would I seem needy? I was so rusty. Dating was something I no longer allowed myself, and it showed because I had no idea how to act.

Once more, from the safe distance keeping us apart, I gave the handsome stranger a slow once-over, relishing each of his features. I wanted nothing more than to run my fingers through his hair, to feel the stubble against my skin, and to sense the power of him by my side.

My skin tingled.

New sensations invaded my senses.

My insides heated up when he cocked his head and our eyes locked. Even from where he stood, his magnetism got to me and swept me off my feet. And we hadn't even exchanged a word yet. Somehow, the way he glanced at me calmed my nerves. It soothed my body and soul. How could someone I'd never met have that much effect on me? It made no sense. But I didn't want to dissect any of it because I loved how my body reacted to his undivided attention.

How, with just a look my way, this man could quiet the voices that that had kept me small for so long. The ones whispering that I wasn't enough, that I didn't deserve more.

The man sipped on his drink, and my gaze trained on his sexy throat as he swallowed the amber liquor. Could a throat be sexy? His was. It never occurred to me to think of it that way. But wow. That man. He had a way of messing with my hormones on a stellar level, and a glance was all we'd shared so far.

Men in suits? Not really my type. Usually. But him…

Men radiating that kind of confidence? No way. Yet somehow…

Men who made my skin tingle with a single glance? Never before. But then…

Until him.

Never looking away, he ambled in my direction. I might have stopped breathing for a full minute. It'd been a while since I had gone out, but even then, I rarely got on the radar of such a man. His entire demeanor screamed charisma. And power. A contrast to the glint illuminating his irises and the small bend of his lips that gave him a boyish appearance. The mix of both made him look irresistible. Way more than it should.

I sent him a shaky nod as his focus burned holes in my skin and put my dress on fire, his stare never wavering from me.

I held my breath. Again. Because how could I fill my lungs with air when it craved his scent?

The man placed his half-filled glass on the plate and grabbed two champagne flutes from a server, erasing the distance between us as he weaved through the crowd.

My body temperature increased as the space between us shrunk.

My knees wobbled when he reached me, but I straightened my back, not wanting to show him how only his presence affected me.

With a smile, I accepted the champagne he offered.

"To a great night and even greater company," he said clinking his glass with mine. "I'm Riley."

Even the sound of his voice was divine. Dripping hot honey, I wished I could have it directed toward me all the time.

Breathing in to calm the butterflies fluttering in my stomach, I met his hand halfway. "I'm Devon." The contact of our palms shot a bolt of electricity through me. One powerful enough to brand its way through me.

To escape the heat sizzling between us, I tried to casually squirm my hand from his, not sure how my body could react so strongly to a stranger, but Riley lifted our joined hands and kissed my knuckles.

Okay, none of this could be real. Who wooed a woman with the gallantry of a gentleman? That was an art long gone—or I believed it had—until now.

A breathless chuckle left me as I watched him. "I can already tell you're a gentleman."

Riley's gaze landed on mine, taking away my breath at its intensity. "My mama taught me well. So, what brings you here, Devon? I've never seen you at one of these country music parties before."

"Oh, you go to these a lot? This is my first time. It's quite intimidating. A friend of mine invited me, but she's running late." I hoped my simple answer could quench his curiosity. Riley didn't need to know how I scored an invite here. This would ruin the moment we shared.

The conversation flew easily between us. As if we'd met before. And we rekindled a friendship after spending time apart.

Riley pointed to a tall man with broad shoulders and a panties-melting grin when he caught us watching him.

Oh yes. Nicole had said famous people would be here, and I thought I recognized him earlier. But since then, my attention had been so riveted to the man in front of me that I failed to notice anyone else.

My eyes rounded at the sight of the man standing a bit further from us.

"Is that Carter Hills? I'm sorry. I'm not a groupie, I swear, but I thought I recognized him earlier when I walked in."

"Yeah, that's him. I can introduce you later."

The last thing I needed was for anyone to know I was here. To be recognized. Or spotted. Nicole thought going out with a bunch of strangers surrounded by a high level of security would allow me a night out without having to watch over my shoulder for once. I agreed because I really needed to escape the confines of my apartment. And live a little. And also feel like a twenty-four-year-old for a night.

Riley watched me, and I felt the warmth pooling in my cheeks. With a headshake, I whispered, "No, you don't have to. I'm nobody here. I'm not part of this world. This night is surreal, I—"

A waitress with a tray full of wine glasses bumped into him, cutting short our conversation. For a split second, I relished the interruption. I needed time to think.

I had no idea how to justify my presence if Riley's interest in me grew and he asked questions I couldn't answer.

My lips pursed, then opened in shock, when in slow motion, the waitress's tray flipped, and wine-drenched his suit.

"Oh, shit. I'm…I'm so sorry. It's…oh gosh, it's my first night here. I'm so, so sorry. I-I messed up. Wh-what can I do?" the waitress asked, her voice shaky and eyes brimming with tears.

I watched their exchange as Riley comforted her with his words and even offered her a job if she decided waitressing wasn't her thing. Everything he said only increased my attraction to him, and I could already tell he was selfless and caring.

His next words froze me in place, sending an emotional surge through me—one I hadn't felt in almost a decade. "Don't worry. The sun always comes out after the storm."

I sank deep into my memories, losing myself in the past.

My mother used to say those same exact words to me a lot growing up. Every time dark shadows hovered over us and I needed a little faith that everything would be all right. A reason to keep going. Only now did I understand. She needed those words even more than I ever had. She held onto them, hoping they'd find their way into her heart and make sense of her world. For her sake. And maybe for mine, too.

The last time I saw her, she came to my bedroom and hugged me. Every time she and Harry fought, I shrank into myself, trying to be as small as possible. Fear wrapped around me like a blanket, and I always felt completely alone. I think she knew. This time, it hadn't turned physical, but it still cracked the foundation of the little girl I had been. She had brushed her fingers through my hair, just as she had since I was a small child, murmuring those words over and over as I lost myself in her loving embrace.

"I love you, baby. And don't worry. The sun always comes out after the storm. Never forget it." I didn't know at the time she was giving me a piece of life advice, as if she knew it would be the last time. Those were her last words to me. And I'd never forgotten them.

In the past few years, I'd held on to the words but lost the hope they once carried, too busy fighting for my own life, more than once. But hearing them now from Riley's lips hit me like a freight train. As if my mom were still watching over me, reminding me she was here, in my corner, cheering for me in her own quiet way.

The waitress left with her chin high and confidence drumming her steps as I stood there speechless, my eyes following her.

Once she disappeared into the crowd, I leaned closer to Riley. His generosity. His calm. His gentleness. His way of lifting the spirit. None of it went unnoticed. It all spoke of his character. And I really liked what I'd just witnessed.

"Wow. That was... That was amazing. Most people would have screamed at the poor girl or threatened to get her fired. Instead, you boosted her self-confidence. That's very noble of you. You are a good man, Riley."

He pinched the fabric of his wet shirt. "Thank you. It was just a clumsy mishap. Now, would you excuse me for a minute? I need to freshen up."

I smiled at him, because even stained in red wine, that

man looked effortlessly handsome. And it appealed to me. Every cell of me.

With a nod and a smile, I offered to order more drinks. His eyes lit up when I mentioned whiskey.

Would he notice I had observed what he was drinking before we even met?

I didn't want to sound too obvious, but at the same time, I wished he could see I wasn't indifferent to him. That I saw him. Like he saw me.

Fire burned between us. Hotter by the minute.

Our eyes locked. I didn't want him to walk away. For a reason I couldn't explain, I felt safe around him. As if no harm could get to me…or find me.

I grinned like a fool at his retreating back.

My heart danced in my chest. It felt lighter than it had been in so long. Perhaps I, too, was entitled to greater things in life than what I'd experienced until now.

The sun always comes out after the storm.

How could he have known? Unless we were destined to meet tonight. Unless our encounter wasn't just random, but life sending me a message. Maybe there was something between us…something to share that neither of us yet understood.

Feeling as if I were floating, gravity unable to hold me down—and as if the sun were finally breaking through after years of stormy skies—I waltzed to the nearest bar.

A chill crawled down the length of my back, and the air around me grew heavy before I even saw him. Darkness coiled around me like a ribbon of thorns.

A death grip clutched my elbow from behind, and I yelped in pain.

All my hopes vanished, replaced by a feeling of dread. And creeping fears.

"Well, well, well. I never thought I'd find you here. I

must say, you impress me, Devon. How you scored an invite to this party is beyond me." His cruel voice was the very echo of my nightmares. "The fun is over. Time to go back where you are safe. We're leaving."

The air halted on its way to my lungs. Tears prickled the back of my eyes.

How did he find me? He had no way of knowing I would be here. I'd been careful. I had made sure to take a cab and to leave no clues in my apartment about where I was headed. Unless…Nicole. Did he get to her? Or follow me? No. The couldn't be. These people weren't his usual crowd. How on earth had he landed an invite? Still, when it came to him, nothing seemed impossible.

All night, I'd been careful not to draw any attention to myself. But somehow, I'd failed. My night of freedom was about to backfire. Again. And the consequences would be catastrophic…for me. Soon, my body would bear the marks of the price I paid for a few stolen hours of respite.

A giant stone blocked my airways. Every fiber of my being was aware this wouldn't end well and the pain would be more than just physical.

As discreetly as possible, I scanned the bar, hoping I'd see Riley on his way back. Or anyone who could help me. In vain. I was invisible here. I didn't belong in this world. Nobody even knew my full name. Not even the man I ached to see again.

I tripped on my heels as Robbie led me away, his iron grip on my elbow never loosening.

Steel bands coiled around my stomach. I blinked to keep the tears building in the corners of my eyes at bay.

I refused to show any sign of weakness in front of him. Never. This was one of the few things I still had control over.

Acting like a caring husband who was helping his

drunk wife find her balance, Robbie circled my waist with a firm grip, holding me flush against his body, rigid with anger. His fingers bit into the soft flesh of my side, certain to leave bruises.

The sun always comes out after the storm.

Maybe my mother was wrong all along. There were only storms. No sunshine.

Chapter 3

Returning to the party in my damp suit, I scanned the crowd for the woman in the red dress.

My eyes traveled around the place, but Devon was nowhere to be seen.

Perhaps her friend had arrived, and she went to greet her.

I closed my eyes and racked my brain. Minutes ago, she had told me she'd get us more drinks. My gaze wandered to the bar section of the rooftop, and I side-stepped to get a better view. No sign of her there either.

Perhaps she had to use the ladies' room. I was in no rush. There was nowhere I'd rather be, so I'd wait for her to return.

Aisha Jones waved at me from a distance and mouthed *I'll call you tomorrow* in my direction. I gave her a thumbs-up, and a large smile broke free on her face. The kid was doing great.

She was the latest artist I'd signed under my management, and I knew from the start that both of us would do incredible things together. The girl had been in the music industry since she was a kid and was fearless. She possessed a rare talent.

Call it some big brother's instinct, but I wanted to watch over her now that she'd embarked on a solo career and help take her to the top.

We broke eye contact as Carter walked to me and swung an arm across my shoulders. From his six-foot-five height, he towered over me by half a foot.

"Hey man," he said, sliding another tumbler of whiskey into my hand.

With a nod, I raised it to thank him.

"I thought your woman would be here tonight?" I asked, tipping an eyebrow.

Carter's eyes filled with tenderness. And love. They always did every time someone mentioned his wife, the woman who'd vacationed in the cabin next to his one winter and broke the walls around his icy heart, replacing it with warmth. "She wanted to come but is in bed with a bad case of flu." He took a sip of his water—Carter Hills drank no alcohol. Never. "Who was the woman in the red dress you were talking to earlier? She had sparks in her eyes when she looked at you. And so did you. Even from where I was standing, I could tell. I know firsthand you're a difficult man to impress, Riley Burns. I know that from spending years by your side on and off tour. So, tell me, are you two together?"

"Nah, I just met her. Her name's Devon. She's sweet and gorgeous. She has a little something I can't resist. I don't think she knows how beautiful and enticing she is." I scanned all around us, trying to spot her in the crowd. No sign of her. Did she leave? No. Impossible. We hit it off.

Easy conversation. Lots of smiles and eye contact. Yeah, she'd be back.

Carter emptied his glass in one gulp. "I need to go. I told my wife I'd make it home before midnight. She's probably asleep by now, but I want to be with her anyway."

"Are you staying at your penthouse or driving back to the mountains tonight?"

"Penthouse. We'll drive back to Green Mountain tomorrow." Carter clapped my shoulder. "And by the way, nice suit. If you're trying to start a new fashion trend, you might be onto something. Riley's Custom Undershirts. Yeah, that could work. If you decide to go through with it, I'll even offer my services as a model. Or an investor. I have faith in you, man. Always."

I wrinkled my nose and nudged him in the ribs. "Laugh all you want, Country Man," I mocked his back as he walked away, shoulders shaking.

Yeah, so funny.

I lifted my glass to my lips and nodded at Thomas Barlow, a friend of my father, when a movement in red closing in on the elevator caught my eyes.

Devon.

I moved through the crowd. The density of it made it impossible to rush to her fast enough. The air in my lungs turned to ice. A prickly sensation tickled the nape of my neck. From across the room, my eyes took her in as she entered the elevator car, a man with broad shoulders and a dark crewcut manhandling her. Everything else around me vanished from my sight. Only Devon mattered. And her safety. I discarded my tumbler on the nearest table and clenched my hands at my sides, feeling helpless as the jerk pushed her forward. A gasp left my mouth when she tripped over her heels. The man caught her before she could fall face first.

By her side, the man towered over her, his stare cold and threatening.

I bumped into more people as I hurried in their direction.

The man shoved her forward once more, and she turned around, our gazes colliding. Her face falling. My heart cracking.

Devon had lost her spark. Now she looked pale, and scared. The fight hadn't left her, though. Her gaze was a mix of resolve and fire. Whoever that man was, she was aware he was bad news but refused to give him the satisfaction to abide by his commands.

With a tilt of his head, the man lowered his mouth to her ear and said something that made her go rigid. The primal fear shadowing her face killed a piece of my heart, even at this distance. There was something so raw about it. Devon schooled her features, her lips now pressed into a thin line to stop them from trembling, her back straight.

It wasn't the first time she'd been handled that way by him. I could tell. She knew this game, all too well.

My pulse thumped in my ears. "Come on, people. Move," I said at no one, as I approached her.

Every hair on my back stood on end.

My breathing hitched as if I'd just run ten miles at full speed.

Time slowed.

My throat worked.

An emotion I'd never felt before filled me. Helplessness.

Devon raised her eyes in my direction. I stopped in my tracks. We watched each other for a few seconds. I wished she could read the worry on my face. Before I could do anything else, she gave me an *I'm so sorry* glance, then dropped her gaze as the elevator doors slid shut between us.

For a long second, I froze. Unable to move forward.

Every alarm in my head screamed its warning. Something wasn't right. Whoever that man was, danger radiated from him.

As soon as I regained control of my body, I surged forward.

In my hurry, I shoved people aside and reached the elevator thirty seconds too late.

Like a kid in a department store, I jabbed the button repeatedly, cursing under my breath.

I scratched my neck, my throat tightening with rising panic.

That man was as good as dead if he thought hustling women was acceptable. There was no way I'd let him get away with it.

The look in Devon's eyes would haunt me—fear, submission, acceptance.

I dragged a hand over my face. This was bad.

I closed my eyes, trying to remember if there was a band on her ring finger. No. None. The only jewels she wore had been a square ruby ring on her right middle finger, a delicate bracelet on her left wrist, and little heart-shaped gold earrings.

I battered the elevator button with my palm now. Fuck, why was it taking so long?

For a moment, I considered taking the stairs down forty-one floors, but I quickly dismissed the idea. No way I'd make it on time, even if I sprinted.

Running out of ideas to reach the lobby faster, I dialed Carter. Maybe he hadn't left yet. "Hey. Are you still here?"

"Yeah, halfway across the lobby right now. What's wrong?"

I inhaled through my mouth to calm the blazing bundle of nerves barreling in my stomach. "You know the woman? Devon? She entered the elevator with some dickhead…and I don't know, man. She looked scared as shit. He's bad news." I forced a breath out. "Can you keep an eye out for her? I'll be down as soon as the stupid car reaches the rooftop. Thanks, man." I hung up before he could utter another word.

I clenched and unclenched my fists at my sides.

"Fucking finally," I muttered under my breath as the elevator doors slid open.

The descent to the lobby felt endless. I counted each floor backward as the elevator crept down, my patience unraveling with every number.

Carter met me as soon as I exited the suffocating box, my body tense and my breathing fast and uneven.

"Have you seen her?"

My friend shook his head. "No. She never exited the elevator. I'm sorry. I wish I could do something more."

I huffed and dropped my shoulders. "Thanks for trying. I'll stay here a little longer, see if she comes through those doors at some point."

"Do you want me to stay with you?" my friend asked. "Think the guy's her husband?"

Something inside me told me he wasn't. "No, but she was afraid of him. I could tell. She had lost all her spark. As if she knew she was condemned to a death sentence. It's bad. Call it a hunch, but I know I'm right about this."

Carter cleared his throat and nervously rubbed the sole of his shoe against the tiled floor. "Do you think she's like a…an escort? That he could be her pimp or something? Or her handler? We've seen all kinds of women crashing our parties, looking for a paid fuck before." He offered me an apologetic glance.

I raked my fingers through my hair, not bothered about messing it up anymore.

"No. Hell no. Could he…could she? No. *No, no, no.* She didn't have that vibe. She doesn't fit the profile. I'm telling you something was off with that guy. If she were here for the money, he wouldn't have forced her to leave. No, it's something else. I can tell. Devon was genuine. She even refused to meet you. All women chasing fame and money want to meet you, man. No offense, but it's true. That should be all the confirmation we need."

Carter seemed to think. "Yeah. You're probably right. And the way she looked at you… It wasn't with that kind of interest. You guys had blazing chemistry. Even I could tell. Sorry for asking."

"Don't be. We're always looking out for each other. I'm okay with you worrying sometimes."

"What do we do now? Should we search the building?"

Carter said *we* because we were that kind of team.

It was my turn to clap his shoulder. "Nah. Go back to your wife. I'll be fine. I'll call you tomorrow. Keep you updated."

"You sure? She would understand if you needed me. April loves you, you know. So, don't worry about it."

I sighed. "Nah, you carry on. I meant what I said. I can watch for Devon on my own. Go home. Say hello to April for me. I hope she knows I love her too. Next time you're in town, let's get together. I miss you guys."

Carter eyed me for a long moment. "Okay, then. Will do. Good luck, Ry. Keep me in the loop. And call me if you change your mind."

———

The next morning, I entered my house at ten. I'd spent my entire night at the hotel, trying to catch sight of Devon.

I'd pulled in all my contacts to get the guest list—her

name wasn't on it—and since I never learned her friend's name, this was a dead end.

In the security booth, I looked at the surveillance videos until I was blurry-eyed.

No trace of her. Or the man. It was like she never existed. As if I'd imagined her.

She'd vanished into thin air, leaving no clue on how to reach her, no last name to track her down, no trace to follow.

Defeated, I undressed—my clothes still reeked of old red wine—and fell face first on the bed, not taking the time to shower beforehand. God, I probably looked as much of a mess as I felt.

The night had been long. So damn long. I might have drunk ten cups of coffee and three power drinks to stay awake.

All for nothing.

Still, Devon's disappearance and the way that man manhandled her didn't sit well with me. My gut told me she was in trouble. That she needed someone's help. *My* help. And right now, I had no way to save her—or even know if she was all right.

Deep down, I wondered if she needed saving at all. Was this the kind of situation? Was her life truly in danger, or was her safety at risk?

Fuck, I had no clue.

A chill ran through me.

Deep inside, I hoped I was wrong. That I'd misread the situation. And her terror. But from the way it all went down, I was pretty sure I'd come to the right conclusion. Devon didn't choose to leave last night. She was compelled to.

From the look of it, I would never know what

happened. And I could tell the mystery of her disappearance would haunt me for a very long time.

Sleep called to me. My eyelids weighed heavier with each passing second.

Too tired to analyze the situation any further, I shut my burning eyes and fell asleep in no time, dreaming of the woman whose full name I longed to know.

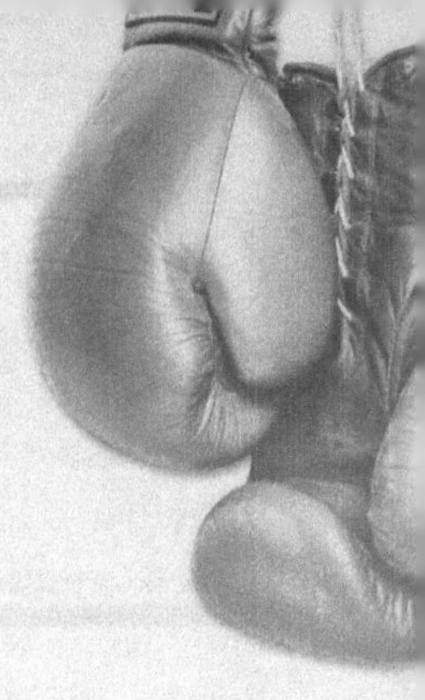

Chapter 4
Devon

Thirteen years ago

High-pitched screams filled the house. Even though I should be accustomed to them by now, I was not. They still pierced my heart every time they cleaved the silence. I closed the door of the bathroom and heaved out my breakfast, my hands clamping the toilet seat in desperation with chills running through me. I slumped against the wall, my fingers sore, my mind tired, unable to block the cries of pain. Growing up, I thought love was magical. And healed everything. Fairy tales before bed were my favorites. I used to imagine I was the princess, rescued by her knight, falling in love, and living happily forever. In a castle. With bunnies. And a horse named Johnny. The end. Yes, those were what my childhood dreams were made of.

Until reality hit me at age seven.

My birth father left my mom when she was three months pregnant. Never looked back. Never asked to meet me or sent birthday cards. My mother met him at a bar. They dated for a few months, and I was the surprise that came from the not-so-serious relationship. More a shock to him. From what she told me—and it took me years to break through her walls and get even a glimpse into her story—he was a drunk who used to hit her every time he drank too much. Yes, that kind of a jerk.

I didn't need him in my life. Better off. That I understood early on.

Mom and I were good on our own. I was her little princess, and she was my hero. We weren't rich by any means, but she loved me. With every chunk of her heart.

And it was worth more than anything money could ever buy.

I was happy. We were happy. And life was good.

Then she met Harry. He was a devoted single dad to his only son, Robbie. From baseball practices to teaching him everything he knew about mechanics, Harry's whole world rotated around his little boy.

One day, my mother's car broke down on the interstate, and a man came to her rescue. Like in a fairy tale, he swept her off her feet. Her own hero driving a white car.

My mother and Harry fell in love and got married six months later.

Harry was everything my dad had never been. Caring. Funny. Generous. Present. And he loved my mom. Like crazy.

Robbie became my big brother the moment we first met. He was a few years older than me and had taken the role of the hero in my life.

Until I would be old enough to meet my own knight in shining armor.

Robbie looked out for me. He prepped my favorite breakfast in the morning. He warned off the boys messing with me at school—and the naughty girls too.

My friends all loved him. I loved him. He was my everything.

After the wedding, Harry adopted me officially, and the four of us became a real family. *The Millers.* The one I had always dreamed of. It was as if the universe had heard my prayers and made all my dreams come true.

White picket fence. Backyard with a swing set. Matching PJs on Christmas morning. We were only missing a dog to be a picture perfect family.

Yeah, we were that kind of happy.

Maybe I wanted to believe in fairy tales so much that I had been blind to the signs. Or perhaps my childhood innocence was to blame.

I should've known better than to believe it could all be true.

My trip down memory lane faded as more screams vibrated through the house, and I was brought back to the present. I put my palms over my ears to muffle the sounds. I hummed to myself so that the only thing I could hear was my own voice.

Every cell in me cried from fear.

Another wave of nausea hit me, and I emptied my stomach in the toilet bowl again. Scorching tears burned my eyes. The lining of my throat felt like a trail of fire.

Loud steps resonated on the other side of the door.

I started shaking, and I wasn't even cold.

My body just couldn't handle the panic anymore, or the helplessness that always came with moments like this.

I braced myself, closed my eyes, and held my breath.

If I kept silent, maybe he wouldn't realize I was in here.

Someone turned the doorknob, and my lungs went on strike. I was afraid any sound—even my own breathing—might give me away. I shut my eyes and prayed no one was coming for me, that I was safe from harm. I uttered the tiny prayer I'd come up with, every time I felt my heart would jump out of my chest and never return, and waited, not entirely ready for what would happen next.

Warm hands clutched my shoulders, and a soft voice spoke close to my ear.

"Hey, Devon. It's me. I'm here now. Don't be afraid, okay? I'll take care of you. Everything will be all right. Remember what I told you to do when this happens?"

I opened my eyes, swallowed the giant lump in my throat, and jumped into Robbie's arms. Where I knew I'd be out of harm's way. My brother—stepbrother—would never let anything bad happen to me. He would always protect me. Care for me. He was my hero, and heroes never failed their mission.

The steady rhythm of his heart against my ear decreased the crazy beating of mine.

I buried my face in his chest, relishing the fresh laundry scent of his T-shirt as his hand drew circles on my back.

"I'm here now. You're safe."

You're safe.

I loved hearing those words. But I also knew deep down it wasn't normal for a kid to hear them so often.

Robbie cradled my face, wiping the tears running down my cheeks with his thumbs. "It's okay, Devon." His gaze shifted to the toilet. "Have you been sick again?"

I nodded, looking down, ashamed of not being able to get a grip on myself. To have no control over my mind or body. Or my fears.

The sound of my mother's cries reached my heart.

Then a door closed with a loud bang.

More wails echoed through the quiet.

Robbie whispered, "It's you and me, okay? We can get through this. I have your back."

He rocked me back and forth, his voice the only thing I focused on. The only thing I required right now.

My brother was my safe place. He was my haven whenever the storm came knocking.

—————

Eight years ago

The phone rang, but my brain couldn't comprehend where the sound came from. Was it a dream? My thoughts were foggy. I shifted on my bed, relishing the warmth of my comforter as I dozed off again.

A hushed voice pulled me out of my slumber.

For a moment, I thought it was another dream.

A hand shook my shoulder.

A beam of light pierced my closed eyelids.

I tried to rouse myself from my sleep as the low voice spoke again. Closer this time.

In my semi-consciousness state, I couldn't make out the words spoken to me.

A hand jiggled me gently again, and my brain woke up.

"Devon."

I recognized my brother's voice.

"Let me sleep, Robbie. It must be like two in the morning. I have a math test tomorrow."

"Devon. It's about your mom. And Harry."

Robbie never called his father dad. He always used his

first name. He once said to me it was easier to pretend it was a stranger kicking him in the ribs when he was younger than knowing his own dad could do something that horrible to him.

The beating stopped after Harry married my mother. She became his sole victim.

The victim of his hatred.

The victim of his fury.

The victim of everything bad happening in his life—and there was plenty of that.

Mom would take any beating Harry gave her if it meant saving Robbie and me from the same fate. Even at the risk of her own life.

Harry never touched me. Not once. He never even yelled at me.

He called me his precious child. His sweet daughter. The apple of his eyes.

Deep down, I was afraid he would change his mind about me one day, and I'd become another one of his victims. After all, he wasn't much different from my biological dad. The only difference was that Harry didn't need booze to turn into a monster.

"What about them?" I grumbled. They were gone until Friday, and selfishly, I thought I could finally breathe for two days without fearing for my life. Since our parents had gone to a cabin with Harry's co-worker, I knew my mom would be safe for those two days too. No way Harry would let anything slip if there were people around. Nah, he would not break the image of his poster-perfect marriage in front of people. Never.

He loved showing off my mom around too much. She was like his prized possession. A trophy wife. The shiny toy he paraded around. Until he closed the front door of our home at night. Then she became his prey.

But Harry was a smart man and never hurt her where it showed. My mother's face never got any bruises or cracked lips. Her ribs were another story, though. And her thighs.

Right now, I was deep in sleep, making up for all the nights I'd kept one eye open, just in case Harry decided to give me a taste of his women-beating medicine. That day would come when I fell out of his grace. Until then, I would grow stronger than my fear—without letting it own me. I wouldn't be reduced to my anxieties. That wasn't my endgame.

"Devon… it's important."

I frowned as Robbie's voice washed over me.

My brother sucked in a deep breath. "Th-they had an accident. A moose. They're fighting for their lives. We need…we need to get going. The hospital is an hour's drive from here." His voice cracked on the last word. "I'm sorry. About…huh…about your mom. Harry deserves to die. I hope he dies. She never should have married the man. He-he's toxic. But I'm here, okay? Forever. I'll take care of you. No matter what. You are my family, Devon. Only you. You can count on me. I'll never abandon you. We'll always be together."

Tears built in my eyes but refused to fall.

I ran my hands over my face, trying to make sense of everything my brother just said.

My mother. A moose. Accident. Hospital.

This all seemed surreal right now.

Robbie clutched my upper arms and helped me sit. "Devon, did you understand anything I said?" he asked, searching my gaze in the dim-lit room.

I nodded. And nodded again.

"Yeah. My…my mom had an accident. We have to

go." I blinked. "Gimme five minutes, I'll meet you in the car."

As if I'd turned into an automated, emotionless robot, I put sweatpants and a hoodie on, knotted my hair in a messy bun, and slid my feet into sneakers I left by the front door.

Robbie said nothing as I climbed into the car next to him. He knitted his fingers through mine, and I closed my eyes, tilting my head back, and chasing away the thought of my mother's accident—and her life hanging by a thread—as far away as possible. Now wasn't the time to be weak. She needed my strength. And my prayers. She needed my courage and my love.

"I'm here, okay?" Robbie whispered, his voice tender. "We'll be fine with or without them. I'll watch over you. Always. Make sure you're safe and sound. You'll never be alone. You're all I have left."

I inhaled, fighting the fresh batch of tears pooling in my eyes.

Safe. I didn't realize how much I yearned to hear him say that until the words passed his lips. Safety felt like such a foreign concept most of the time.

"Th-thanks."

We didn't say anything for the next hour.

At seven the next morning, the doctor came to see us. I was lying on a row of hospital chairs, my head propped on my brother's lap as he twisted strands of my hair around his fingers, while I fell in and out of sleep.

The entire time, he repeated we'd be all right. And I really wanted to believe him, but deep down, something told me nothing would ever be okay again if my mom died.

"I'm sorry, but your father passed a couple of minutes

ago. There was nothing we could do. He had a perforated lung, and his spinal cord was crushed."

Robbie straightened and pushed me into a sitting position beside him. I held to his hand like a lifeline as the doctor delivered the news.

We both bobbed our heads as he kept talking. But I registered nothing. Not a word. All my thoughts drifted to my mother. Would she still be alive at the end of the day? I couldn't lose her. I needed her. She was my very first hero. Heroes didn't die in a car crash. Not with a moose. They fought back. They fought with everything they had to save their lives. They survived.

Harry had been hitting her for years. Before him, my sperm donor had done it too. Through it all, she survived. She was a fighter. Stronger than any of us. If someone could go through a deadly car crash, it was her.

After everything she'd endured over the years, she deserved her own happy ending. Her happily-ever-after. True love. Her own hero to deliver her from her hell.

Robbie's arm draped around my shoulders. His voice brought me back. "What about Karen? Did she pull through the surgery?"

The doctor's voice reached my ears this time. "It's too early to tell. She's stable now but in a coma. We should know more in the next few hours. I hope. Hang on, kids. We're doing our best." He cleared his throat. "I'm sorry for your loss."

"Don't be," Robbie barked. "He was a wife-beater. The guy earned everything happening to him tonight."

The doctor's eyes widened, but he said nothing. "We'll keep you informed as soon as we know more."

"Can we see her?" I asked, my voice shaky and barely audible.

"Not right now. Give her some time. She's in ICU. She

needs a lot of rest and care. We'll come to get you as soon as possible."

I held my breath for a beat, trying to calm the nausea swirling in my empty stomach.

"Please, mom. Don't leave me. Don't leave us. We need you. You're free now," I muttered to myself, hoping any saint, god, or divinity up there could hear my prayer and save my mother from her deadly fate.

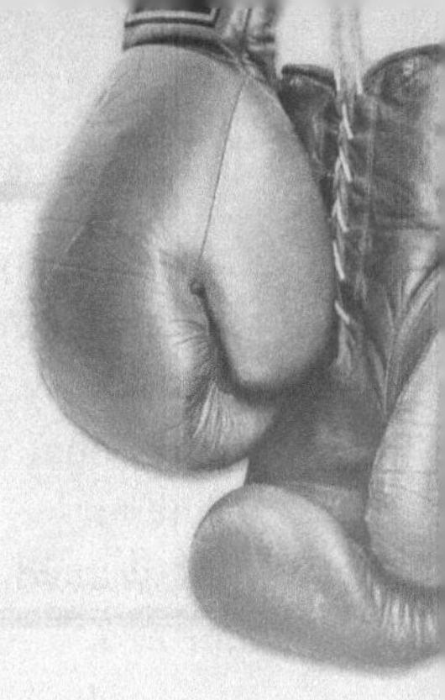

Chapter 5

Devon

Present

"Let go, Robbie. You're hurting me." My stepbrother pushed me inside the elevator car, clamping his fingers on my upper arm, sure to leave more bruises, his stare burning my skin. Robbie and I used to be close. Brother and sister. Best friends. Not quite. Not anymore.

Something happened in his life that made him like this. Hard and violent. Heartless and furious. Like his father.

Did Krista divorce him three years ago because he hit her too?

How would I know? Once the papers were signed, she moved out of state, and nobody had seen her since.

She was like a big sister to me. We got along great. If my stepbrother ever hurt her, she never confided in me. The thought that she might have gone through the same pain filled my heart with unbearable sorrow. Fury, anger, dread, and grief swirled inside me, a turbulent cocktail I could barely contain. Would this hell be my life forever? Was I doomed to the same abuse my mother had suffered before me?

I wanted to cry, but that well had dried up a long time ago.

I wanted to scream, but no sound came out.

I wanted to fight back, but years of experience had taught me it would be pointless—and that I'd end up hurt far more than he would.

I wanted to run away, but through the years, I'd learned Robbie always found me. No matter where I hid. He had eyes everywhere. People on the lookout for me. That was how this whole thing started. Because one of his dear friends opened his mouth about my whereabouts, and it got me in trouble. Now I was an easy prey because he watched me—all the time. Morning and night. I had no way out. I tried. And tried. Several times. But it always ended up with another round of beating. Worse than the previous one.

From an outsider's point of view, Robbie was a selfless brother, caring for his little orphan sister. Pure hero material. Only I knew the truth. He was the devil reincarnated—not the hero I had always pictured him to be.

I steeled myself for the violence about to crash down on me again, ready to shatter me. It was never just about broken bones. Well, it was...but it also went far beyond physical pain. This kind of abuse stilled something deep inside me. It scarred my soul. If Robbie could have my soul, he would burn it and savor the ashes. I wouldn't give him the satisfaction of knowing how deeply his betrayal wounded me. He might hit me, and I might cry out in pain. He might terrify me, and I might tremble in fear. But this would not define me. I would keep trying—always—to find a way out, a way to end the abuse, to make someone believe me. And to heal. A flicker of my essence still burned deep inside, and I wasn't ready to let it die.

With a swift movement, I jerked my arm free from Robbie's bruising grip, but he only squeezed me harder in response, deliberately marking me. He might consider that as his possession, but those marks would remind me of my few hours of freedom. Of meeting Riley. For an hour, I was just Devon, free to breathe, free to live, free to be happy, away from fear.

But freedom came with a cost. I was aware I had to pay the price. I had just hoped that, tonight, my whereabouts had stayed under the radar. I swallowed a ball of tears blocking my airways, pivoted on my heels, and met Riley's panicked eyes one last time.

Lines of worry appeared as he took in the too-tight hold Robbie had on my arm. He flexed his jaw, and his eyebrows furrowed. At that moment, I would have given everything I owned, even my soul, to spend more time with him, to shore up my happy memories, my barrier against the darkness. I had to fake innocence. I couldn't risk drawing any attention to the man pursuing us. If Robbie got a whiff of him, he'd destroy him. Just to destroy me a little more in the process.

Unable to look away, I stepped forward, Riley's stare powerful enough to draw me in, but Robbie fisted the back of my dress, making it impossible for me to move away from his side.

From the corner of my eye, I caught sight of Riley weaving his way through the crowd, his pace quickening as he closed the distance between us, coming straight toward me. My knight. Maybe he really did exist. Maybe I could find support and be saved after all. I prayed he'd get here in time. I couldn't live like this anymore. Always looking over my shoulder, worrying Robbie would show up each time I went out. That every one of my actions came with deadly consequences.

Riley got closer, his eyes locked on mine, promises swirling in them that I'd be okay. That he'd get to me and end this misery.

My heart exploded into millions of pieces with no way to glue them back together when the elevator doors closed and torched every drop of hope left in me. The pieces sank so deep in my chest that I believed they could end up on the shiny steeled floor, my body bleeding to death.

"Who's the guy?" Robbie asked, tightening his grip on me. I could hear the venom in his voice. How did he become this man? Had he always been like this, simply masking his true self in plain sight? The Robbie I used to know—nice, caring, and loving—had to still be in there somewhere…maybe.

"Nobody," I said, evening my voice so he wouldn't get a glimpse of my fear.

My stepbrother let out a chuckle that froze the blood inside my veins. "Good. You're all I have left in life, Devon. That's why I need to make sure you're safe and sound. Don't ever walk away from me. Don't forget. You don't need distractions. So no boyfriend, you hear me?"

I nodded, keeping my gaze down and head low.

"Good girl."

The elevator opened on the basement level. My stepbrother squeezed my elbow—stronger than he needed to— and led me through a series of hallways and doors until we reached his police cruiser. He looked back and nodded at the security detail. I knew, with that simple gesture, the surveillance tapes would be wiped clean of my presence. My friend or even Riley would never know what had happened to me. With a shake of Robbie's head, I had become a ghost. A short-lived mirage passing through Riley's life.

Robbie pushed me into the passenger seat, and I hit my forehead on the console between the seats. It stung, but I refused to rub the spot to soothe the pain. No way was I going to give him the satisfaction of knowing he'd hurt me. Robbie hoisted himself behind the wheel, and I shifted closer to the door to get as far away from him as possible. The bruises he made tonight would show. He knew it. He wanted them to. Keeping me home was all part of his plan.

"I am not thrilled about your little excursion tonight, sis. I hate it when you leave your apartment. Remove that sour look from your face. I'm only looking out for you. The world is a bad place, you know. Nice girls like you can get hurt." He lowered his voice and smirked, then extended his arm to grab my hand. The same way he had done the night our parents died. And so many times before. "I want you safe. I can't do it if you run around town dressed like this." He motioned to my red dress with a jerk of his chin. "Do you understand?"

I nodded.

I'd learned to agree with everything Robbie said when he was in his protective mode. Pissing him off never ended well for me. That much I knew.

"Great. Now let me drive you home. You need to change. I hate knowing men are looking at you as if you were theirs to play with. Nobody messes with my little sister." He smiled. A crooked tilt of his lips that wrapped my spine in an icy chill.

We rode in silence, the air in the car thick with fear. My fear.

My stepbrother kissed my cheek and dropped me off

on the sidewalk in front of my apartment building. He rolled his window down, and I held my breath, preparing myself for whatever he had to say. "No more parties, do you understand? Stay inside and lock the door. I'll try to swing by after my shift." He winked and drove away.

No, please, no more visits tonight. There was only so much one girl could survive in a single night.

I didn't need to be reminded once again why he was teaching me a valuable lesson when his fist connected with my flesh and bones.

Images of Riley flashed through my mind.

Everything was easy with him. I would remember his warm smile forever. Like a safe haven, shielding me from all this pain. His comforting presence and selfless nature, the way he pursued me when he realized I was in trouble. Their memories would become my comfort in times of storm.

Riley was everything that Robbie wasn't.

A ray of sunshine in the pouring rain.

A star in the darkness.

A glimpse of hope in times of war.

For a minute, I could really picture him as my knight in shining armor. The one about whom I, as a little girl, locked in a castle tower—or rather a violent household— had dreamed about. The one rescuing me from my fate. My very own happy ending.

How could he be anything else? The way he reacted to that clumsy waitress earlier said a lot about him. He wasn't playing a game tonight—he was genuinely caring and kind.

A foolish part of me wished he were here—that he really was my knight in shining armor. That he could love me, believe in me. Because right now, even I struggled to believe in any fate other than the one my violent brother had forced upon me.

Who was I fooling, if not myself? It was time to outgrow my childish fantasies. By now, Riley probably believed Robbie was my pimp or something.

Fresh tears welled up in my eyes.

Bile surged at the back of my throat, and I emptied my stomach behind a bush.

This was my body's response to violence and terror. No matter how much time had passed, I never got used to it. It still shocked me to my core.

With trembling fingertips, I dried the tears rolling down my cheeks, my eyes focusing on the point where I knew Robbie's cruiser had disappeared into the night.

My limbs weighed tons as I staggered up the concrete stairs leading to the front door of my apartment building.

I took the elevator to the fourth floor, too weak to climb the stairs.

Adrenaline had drained from my body, my entire self now heavy and slow.

Once in the safety of my home, I pressed my back against the locked door and let my emotions out, my face buried in my hands and shoulders slumped in defeat.

My back glided against the door, and I crumpled to the floor in a ball, the detritus of my broken dreams disappearing like wisps of smoke.

The tear dam had broken, and I had no idea how to fix it this time—or if I even wanted to fix it. Years of carefully held back emotions erupted.

You're stronger than this, Devon, I repeated to myself.

Don't let Robbie rob you of your heart. And soul.

You're better than this life. You deserve better. You'll find a way out.

Eventually. One day. Keep fighting for a better future. Never stop dreaming.

Riley's words replayed in my head. *Don't worry. The sun always comes out after the rain.* Did my mother, from wherever she was, send him to me tonight? Did she know we would hit it off? Or was I overthinking everything? Now, in the silence of the night, I wished I could believe those words. That they would eventually make sense to me.

Icing my bruises after a long shower, I boiled water to make tea, then sat on the sofa, my legs folded underneath me, cradling the warm mug between my hands.

I checked the time. Midnight.

In one last prayer attempt before going to bed and chasing some much-needed sleep, I closed my eyes.

Robbie, please forget about me tonight. Don't come over later.

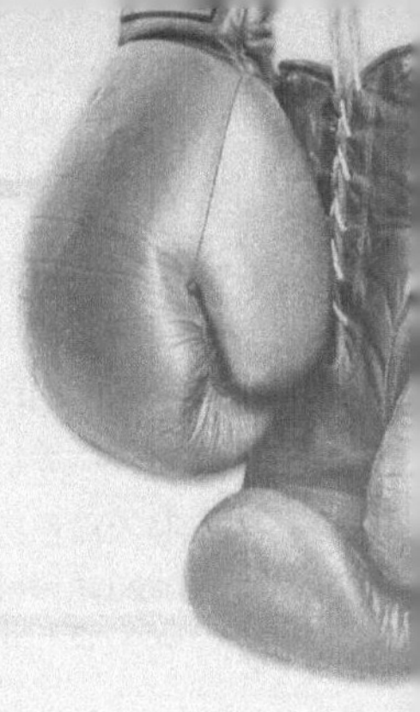

Chapter 6

Riley

How many times had I sat in the same spot over the past six months? More than I could ever count. By now, I knew every single grain in the wood, every scratch and imperfection on the tabletop, and each subtle change in the bar's decor. Not that much ever changed—just the napkins and the servers, really. And most of them I knew by name.

Robert, the bartender, knew my timing too. My drink would already be on the table before I even set foot inside.

I had become that man. Predictable. And obsessed over things I had no control over.

I took a sip from my tumbler while I perused my surroundings, scanning the people coming in and out of the elevator, my usual spot in the hotel bar offering me the perfect view of everyone passing through the lobby.

A couple in their fifties held hands and kissed. At this

pace, I'd be sixty and still single. I chugged the rest of my whiskey and signaled the bartender for more.

After three drinks, the amber liquid didn't burn the lining of my throat anymore. I sighed and rubbed my hands over my face. "What the fuck, Ry." I cursed under my breath, feeling ridiculous.

"Yeah, what the fuck, Ry." Carter echoed my words as he slid his tall self into the seat facing me.

The server put a fresh tumbler before me on the table, grabbing the empty one.

"Water, please," Carter ordered, offering him a tight-lipped smile.

"What are you doing in Nashville, man? You never told me you would be here this weekend. Did we schedule a meeting and I forgot about it?" I fished my phone out of my black leather jacket inner pocket and opened the calendar app. "Nope. No meeting with you for the next two weeks." I raised my eyes to my friend slash client. "What... Wait. How did you find me?"

Carter leaned forward and clapped my shoulder. "C'mon, Ry. I've known you for a long time. You're not as unpredictable as you think you are." I cocked an eyebrow, giving him my most don't-bullshit-me stare. He didn't need to know that being predictable had become my new *modus operandi*. "Okay, maybe June told me about your new hanging spot. She worries about you, man. Says you spend more time here than at the office these days."

"I don't need to explain anything to anybody." Fury boiled inside me. Knots grew in my stomach. Why did everyone think it was okay to stick their noses in my business?

"It's about her, isn't it? The girl in the red dress?" I sipped my drink, trying to hide from Carter's inquisitive stare. "It's me, Ry. You can tell me anything. You've seen me at my worst when Dahlia rejected me. You came to therapy with me when I lost it all. Don't get me started on how I was when April broke up with me or when my brother died. Both times, I was a fucking mess. You were there by my side when I cursed everyone in this life and the next. Each time. So, I'm here, whether you like it or not." He scanned my face and grinned. "Man, got to say, though. I'm not sure this stalker role suits you." He chugged half his glass of water in one gulp.

"Yeah, well… We'll see. I won't stop until I'm certain she's safe and sound. No matter how long it takes."

My insides clenched into a tight ball of nerves as images of Devon's face, shrouded in fear, flashed through my mind.

My friend watched me with a deep frown and raised his palms between us. "Fine. It's your call."

"We must find her, Carter. She's in trouble. I can feel it. Deep in my bones. Help me, okay?" I dragged a hand over my face. "It's messing with my mind…not knowing."

"I can tell, man. Your gut feeling is usually right about stuff. Anyway, when was the last time I said no to you?"

"Thanks, man." A ball of tangled emotions constricted my airways. "I appreciated it."

Carter propped his elbows on the table, seriousness taking over his features. "Tell me what you've got. We'll start from there."

I unfolded the piece of paper I always kept in my pocket and spread it on the table. "Here's what I know so far."

Carter studied it for a moment before bringing his gaze up. "Okay, let's brainstorm. We're pretty unstoppable when we put our heads together." His eyes locked onto mine, studying me for a moment. When he spoke again, his tone softened. "You'll find her, Ry. I feel it. That night, the connection between you two was too strong to be ignored. Don't doubt that life will put her on your journey again. When you least expect it. Even if she has no idea, she's lucky you're watching out for her. No matter the mess she's entangled in, she has you in her corner. And that counts for something."

A dusting of hope settled in me for the first time in months. Yeah, I'd find her. I'd demand the piece of my heart she stole that night back. Only she could provide the missing half.

One day, I'd see Devon again. I made the promise to myself.

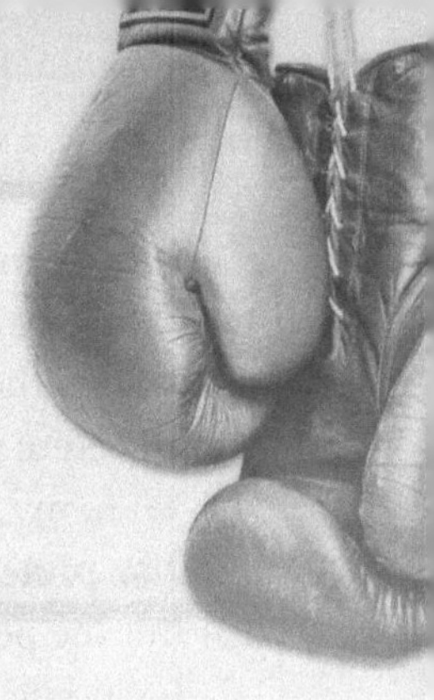

Chapter 7
Riley

In a dark corner of the dive bar, no idea what its name was, I parked my ass for the night and nursed my sixth Tennessee Whiskey, the amount of alcohol circulating in my bloodstream now high enough to prevent me from feeling self-conscious about where I was spending my night. With a flick of my wrist, I swirled the amber liquid in the glass, hypnotized by the half-melted ice cubes clinking at the bottom.

From the outside, my life looked great—almost perfect. Always surrounded by beautiful and famous people. Eating in the best restaurants, chatting with country music superstars and producers who owned half the city of Nashville. I just turned thirty, and thanks to the trust fund my father had set up for me the day I was born and the career I'd built for myself, I didn't have to work a single day in my life if I wanted to.

But that wasn't the point.

I loved my job. I'd basked in country music from the day I was conceived. I could name every country song that played on the radio at age six. And I attended my first award ceremony at nine.

Yeah, my life seemed perfect.

The professional one at least.

But the personal one? Not so much.

Including my love life that was nonexistent.

It was crazy how I could feel so fucking lonely all the time, even with all those people on speed dial.

On the filthy, old wooden table, which had probably seen its share of fights and broken glasses over the year, I stared at my vibrating phone. My mother's face flashed on the screen. I knew the reason. It was those damn calls. I had been ignoring my dad—who I now refused to think of anything more than a sperm donor—for the last two weeks. But my mother? I couldn't disregard her. She knew it. My father knew it. The whole fucking world knew it.

I sucked in a breath, picked up the phone, and pressed the accept button, my elbows resting on the tabletop, my head buried in one hand.

"Hey, Mama," I said, trying to infuse some spirit into my words. My mother had a sixth sense and always knew when I was having a bad day—or a bad month. Yep. She never failed to notice it. Even over the phone.

"Hey, darling. How are you? Your voice is a little off—" As predicted, she'd seen right through me. Or heard as in this case.

"Not much. Having a drink."

"By yourself? Or are you in one of your meetings?"

"Mama, if I were in a meeting, I wouldn't have taken the call. Besides, it's ten at night."

"Oh, you're right. Just checking. Anyway, your father and I will be back in town in a little over a month. We'd like for you to have dinner with us that Saturday. Your father turned fifty-five last week. I want us to celebrate all together… As a family. What do you think?"

I sighed and ran my hand over my face. The idea of seeing my father after our last blow-out didn't sound so exciting right now.

My eyes traveled around the small bar, taking in all the people around me. A man in black chaps was making out with a woman in a sinful red dress, one size too small. I averted my eyes, feeling like a voyeur.

The barmaid, a woman with long black hair and multiple facial piercings, faked being interested in a twenty-something wasted man with braided blond hair, a long beard, and shabby clothes. All for tips. Or maybe he really was her type. Nah—her eyes kept drifting away every few seconds. Nonverbal cues never lie.

And I was there, in a corner, drinking by myself like a real champ.

None of them were people I could interact with—or wanted to interact with, really. Besides, they were all wrapped up in their own lives, without a care in the world for me or my problems.

Damn, what was I even doing here?

"Riley, darling, are you still there?" The sound of my mother's voice, laced with concern, brought my attention back to her.

"Yeah, Mama. Still here. I haven't moved." I lifted the whiskey to my lips and chugged the rest of it. *Thanks, Jack,* I said to myself, raising my glass to the sky. Mr. Daniels had become quite the friend of mine over the past few months —twelve to be exact. We'd always been close, but our friendship had grown stronger since the night Devon disappeared from that rooftop bar.

"Did you hear anything I said? About you coming

home five Saturdays from now? And celebrating your father's birthday?"

"Sure, Mama."

"Can I count on you then? Will you show up, or are you just saying those words to make me think you will?"

I pinched my lips together, swallowing the laugh threatening to come out. How could my mother do this? I bet she'd placed a microchip in my head the day I was born so she could monitor all my thoughts. Yeah, that must have been it.

I moved the phone off my ear and opened the calendar app. It was filled with blue, orange, pink, purple, and yellow squares. My days were full. I was a businessman. Thanks to Carter Hills Band trusting me with their management when they were eighteen and still pretty unknown on the country music scene, I'd become one of the most respected and sought-after managers in Nashville.

Carter Hills Band and I reached stardom together. I had the contacts, the drive—and the big mouth—and they had the talent. A perfect recipe for fame and success.

I scrolled to Saturday five weeks from now. Great. I had no engagement whatsoever that weekend. Nothing. All other weekends for months were booked with events except for that one. I really needed to find that microchip and destroy it as soon as possible. As I stared at my free weekend, I wondered if my mother also had access to my phone. My head fell into the crook of my elbow, and a deep sigh parted my lips.

"I'll come, Mama. Send me the details."

She made a whistling sound—the undeniable sign my mother was pleased. Even if I were tempted to pretend I was busy, I couldn't find it in me to disappoint her.

"Oh, Riley. I'm so happy. We'll have a great time." Her tone turned serious, and she inhaled, noisily enough to annoy me. "And one last thing. Bring a nice lady to join you."

"Mama, I have no one in my life right now—"

"Don't waste your breath, darling. You're surrounded by women every day. I'm sure you can ask someone to come with you. But, please, not a scatterbrained, big-breasted, *I don't know the difference between right and left* woman this time. You almost gave us a heart attack last Christmas. Petula was nice—and probably a great accessory to your star-studded parties—but there wasn't much more she could bring to the table. Bring someone who can hold a conversation."

"Mama—"

"Don't mama me, Riley. I want you to thrive. Always. But you won't have a love life worth mentioning if you act like a five-year-old in a candy store wanting the most colorful sweet when you choose such women to date. You're talented, handsome, and far too intelligent to be that shallow. You have great values and a huge heart… You're one of the most caring people I know. There's more to life than making big bucks and having a great career. Your personal life is just as important. Just think about it."

I rubbed my eyebrow, the liquor in my bloodstream now doing a poor job of numbing my thoughts.

I hated it when my mother's words sounded right. When I didn't have a choice but to let them reach the processing center of my brain and take them into account. I loathed it with every fiber of my being.

I sighed. "I'll think about it." That was the best I could come up with in my intoxicated state. No way I'd promise my mother anything because she'd spend years reminding me what would happen if I brought another *beauty with no brains* woman to their house.

"I love you, honey. Take care. I can't wait to see you.

Don't be a stranger. And please talk to your father. It's time you two make up."

"I will." *Eventually.* I shut my eyes, confident my mother knew I was talking shit. For once, she didn't push the subject and hung up. I exhaled, drained, like I'd just run ten miles.

My stomach churned with all the whiskey I'd drunk tonight.

My mother's voice—even from thousands of miles away—had the kind of power that could cut through the fog of a drinking binge. Almost always enough to sober me up.

I waved over the redheaded waitress in denim cut-offs and a tiny black tank top to bring me the check. She winked at me, and for a moment, I felt self-conscious. She was interested. I wasn't. I placed a hundred on the table and called a cab, in no state to drive the red sports car I'd gifted myself for my thirtieth birthday three months ago.

I faltered out of the cab toward the front porch but dropped my keys before climbing the three steps. In the dark night, my navy-blue craftsman house with stoned columns and white trims looked almost haunted. I scratched the side of my head. Why were the lights out? I had a timer installed when I moved in six years ago. The lights on the front porch turned on at sunset and turned off in the morning. Every single day. No exception.

Not tonight, though. Confusion took my brain hostage. Was there a blackout?

I whirled around on my heels and scanned the street. Every other house had its lights on. I scratched the side of my head again, feeling confusion wrap tighter around my mind.

This was a mystery I'd solve another day. Now all I

craved was a hot shower and a comfy bed to forget all about my week.

I blinked, but my eyes refused to adjust to the darkness. I exhaled sharply and bent down to scramble for my keys. Cold steel met my fingertips. Cold steel met my fingertips. With one hand clamping the banister in a death grip, I barely made it up the stairs before tripping over something, falling to my knees.

"Fucking great."

Had I received a package, and they'd just set it down right in the middle of my way? What a bunch of morons. I squinted, trying to make out what it was, but thanks to the thick veil of darkness, I couldn't see a thing.

These damn lights.

It took my brain a long minute to process the scene and remember the phone in my jacket pocket. With heavy fingers, I switched on the flashlight.

My breath caught in my lungs, and my heart jackhammered in my chest. I tried to scream, but no sound escaped, thanks to my paralyzed vocal cords. What the—? Was it a—? Was it a…body?

I blinked. Yes, the inert form on my front porch was, indeed, a fucking body.

I brought the light beam closer to what looked like a corpse. Ohmygod, was this person dead? My stomach leaped in my throat. Acid filled my mouth. *Don't throw up, man. Think. There had to be an explanation. Don't panic.* Why would there be a dead body on my doorstep? This made no sense. I held my breath, scared the scent of death would penetrate my nose and haunt me forever. My hand shook as I swept the light beam over the still form. The narrow hips and slim legs told me it was either a woman—or a tall child. My stomach twisted. Was this some kind of sick prank? How had a body ended up here, of all places?

Frozen, on all fours, I pondered my options.

As I pressed nine, then one, then one again on my phone, a moan, soft and low, broke the silence. I startled and fell back on my ass. My heart banged against my ribs. Holy crap.

"Riley… Are-are you…huh…Riley?" A woman. The voice belonged to a woman. My shoulders sagged. Okay, no dead people on my conscience. At least, not yet.

I delved into my memories. I knew the voice. I had heard it before. But where? In my state of drunkenness, with alcohol drowning my brain cells, I had a hard time putting a face to the familiar voice.

I cleared my throat. "Huh… That's me. Do-do we know each other?" I must have sounded so stupid right now. For my defense, I'd never had to deal with a left-for-dead body on my doorstep before. "Should I…huh… should I call the police? Are you hurt? Do you need help?" Why was I even asking that question? Of course she needed help. Otherwise, she wouldn't be lying here in the middle of the night.

The woman moved to the side and pushed herself up to sit beside me. A growl of pain escaped her mouth as she wrapped her shaky arms around herself.

Thousands of questions flooded my mind all at once.

I moved closer to catch a sight of her face, trying to avoid blinding her with the light beam.

Gray-blue eyes met mine.

My heart died a thousand deaths in my chest before jolting back to life, beating in a frenzied rhythm.

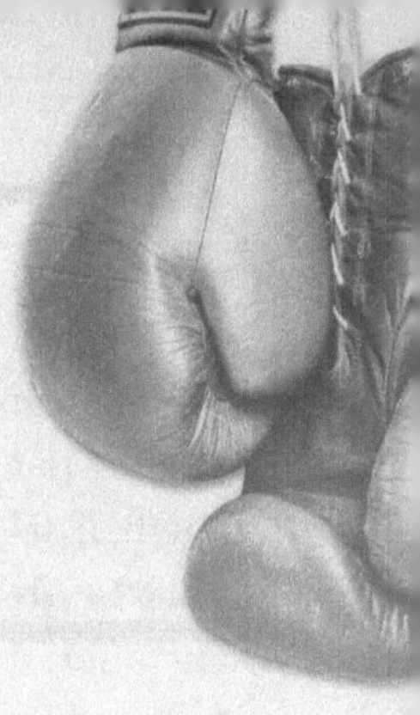

Chapter 8

Devon

I smiled at my computer screen. Today had been a good day. No, scratch that. The entire week had been incredible. I was thriving. Feeling happier than I'd been in a long time. I pressed send on the email intended for one of my clients. He hired me as a freelancing copywriter all year round, providing me with a regular income. Business was booming. In the last two weeks, I'd quoted six jobs and gotten five of them.

Things were finally turning around.

My mother used to say the sun always came out after the storm, and right now I could feel the change in the air. Lately, I'd started to believe her words. Because now they made sense to me.

Robbie had been MIA for weeks, not showing up on my doorstep or following me when I ran errands. Even Mrs. Glifford, my elderly neighbor who lives on my floor, had commented on how cheerful I looked the other day when we left our apartments at the same time.

Not wanting to attract unwanted attention, I usually lay low whenever I ventured out of my home. These days, though, I felt like shining. If my life were a musical, this would be the scene with butterflies and colorful outfits—right after the heroine had defeated the villain and was finally set free.

I knew Robbie would show up again sometime soon. He always did. I bet there was a new woman in his life because that was usually the reason he stopped coming over. It never lasted, though. But for the time being, I would enjoy the freedom his absence provided me.

My fingers lingered on the keyboard of my laptop, and my mind drifted away.

When things got rough, I often wondered if my mother wished for the accident that night. If she hoped her life would end, taking years of pain and suffering along with it. Did she ever think about what my life would become after her death? Did she fear Robbie might turn out to be as much of a monster as his dad, or did she believe I was safe with him watching over me?

When I lie awake at night in the dark, there are so many things I wish I could ask her. My heart cracked in my chest at the mere thought of her.

How many times did I ask myself why she didn't leave Harry after he beat her so badly that she had to miss work for weeks, using migraines as a cover while her cuts and bruises healed that first time?

How many times did I go to sleep hoping she'd be stronger and run away, taking Robbie and me with her?

And now, years later, I was reliving her nightmare. At the hands of the son of the man who tortured her days and nights for as long as I could remember. The man who stained my childhood memories with blood and broken bones.

His son, the overprotective brother I grew up with, had turned into the same kind of monster. Perhaps their demons were contagious. Or hereditary. Could they be? Or did the beating Robbie suffered as a child mess up with a part of his brain and destroy his emotion center? Was it even a thing?

In the last three years, I'd seen many sides of him I'd never witnessed before, and each one gave me worse creeps than the last.

I tried to walk away. I did. Many times. But my stepbrother always found me and brought me back. Every single time. Always pretending it was for my own good. So he could watch over me, just like he promised all those years ago. If I had known…

My phone pinged with a text message.

NICOLE

I miss you. Call me if you wanna chat.

The two sentences brought a smile to my lips.

My fingers itched to dial my best friend, Nicole, to hear her voice, but these days, I tended to stay away from any of the people I cared about. It was my way to protect them from Robbie if he ever landed on their doorstep. If they knew nothing, they were safe—or so I convinced myself.

Nicole and I had been friends since we were teenagers.

She even used to have a crush on Robbie when we were fifteen.

Last year, she invited me to that country music party, and neither of us thought it would end with her nursing a broken wrist after Robbie shoved her against the wall when she refused to tell him where I was.

He threatened my friend so bad that she worried for her own life and gave him the address.

Never again would I endanger my friends just to keep myself safe.

I blew out a long breath and typed,

ME

Not now. Maybe later, okay. Don't worry. I'm fine. I swear. Love you xx

I attached a picture of myself with a thumbs-up just to give her peace of mind.

NICOLE

Oh, you look good, girl. Don't be a stranger, okay? None of this is your fault, D.

ME

I know…

NICOLE

One day, we'll find a way to get you out of this, I promise. I'm sorry it didn't work so far.

ME

I know. Don't blame yourself.

Nicole didn't know the extent of the damages my step-brother had been inflicting on me over the years. I never told her—partly because I didn't want her to worry about me more than she already did, and partly because I knew Robbie would break more than her wrist if she ever tried to step in. Or punish me with his kicks and fists if he found out I'd confided in someone.

Nicole thought he slapped me a few times in the past and prevented me from going out and meeting people. That was true. But she had no idea about all the concussions, broken bones, and hits I'd suffered in the name of what Robbie called family.

As if things weren't bad enough, he was my emergency contact.

I had switched it to Nicole once, but somehow, he got it changed back again. I didn't know how he found out, but somehow, he always got his way. Every time I sought medical help, he ended up being called. I tried telling the ER staff about my wounds once, but Robbie even had friends embedded there, and they reported back to him. Whatever he had on them must have been pretty damn incriminating for them to agree to be his snitches. Or maybe they respected him too much to see any harm in what they were doing. Either way, as a respected cop, Robbie knew how to play the worried-brother card with the doctors. Three times I was beaten so badly we had to change ERs, hopping between hospitals to avoid raising suspicion, managing to convince everyone it had been a car accident. Slipped because I was so damn clumsy. Banged my head after I was mugged in an alley. He was a terrific actor. He won everyone over with his ability to make the injuries believable. Each time, I nodded in agreement and played whatever role my brother pinned on me.

That uniform saved him from trouble far more times than it should have.

A lopsided smile appeared as I stared at the screen, wishing my friend could be here with me, and we'd make plans about meeting guys or going on a vacation, instead of planning an escape. A tightness grew in my chest. Twenty-something girls should dream about the future. Not how to go out without being caught.

With glossy eyes, I re-read Nicole and my text exchange once more before erasing the conversation.

If Robbie ever showed up, I didn't need him going

through my phone and finding another reason to punch me or tug my hair and drag me on the floor.

He had a tendency to do that when I disobeyed his pseudo-rules. Rules he fabricated on the fly and expected me to follow.

Since the day the beating had started, I only wore my hair tied in a braid, then wound as a knot behind my head. This way, it hurt a little less when he pulled at it.

Once, he tugged so hard, strands detached from my scalp, and he discarded them with a wince as if he hadn't just ripped them off. That time, the tears stilled as the pain became unbearable, knotting my insides so tight that not a single emotion leaked out or rolled down my cheeks. It took almost two weeks for the spot on my scalp to stop hurting.

My fingers skimmed the one-inch diameter scar reminding me of that day, and a chill skated up my back.

Last year, I thought about shaving my hair off, but I knew it would just lead to more attacks because Robbie would tell me how ugly it looked. In his twisted mind, he believed women should never sport hair shorter than their shoulders. Fearing he would shake me even more, I refrained.

Anyway, I loved my curls. When I was a little girl, my mother used to say all princesses would be jealous of them. It filled my heart with pride. In a way, my golden locks reminded me of my time with her. When everything seemed possible and my wishes knew no limits.

I held on to them as I still held on to my happily-ever-after dreams.

Without thinking about it, I opened the map app on my laptop and typed the address, firmly etched into my mind. I zoomed in and studied the house for a long minute. This place looked like a safe haven. With a large backyard and trees that provided shade and intimacy.

Craftsman-style exterior.

A white picket fence.

A double-sized driveway with a cobblestones path.

A couple of months back, I'd driven there a few times but never found in me the courage to knock on the wooden front door.

I blew out a cleansing breath and erased my browser history.

I'd become so good over the years at hiding everything I did. It had become second nature to me. Protecting myself and the ones I loved. No matter the cost.

An email popped up on my screen.

Another job order.

I pumped my fist, ready to celebrate.

"Girl, get some champagne," I said to myself. I wished I had people to party with. Friends who'd be proud of everything I achieved by myself, despite the odds.

I blinked the emotions threatening to put out the fireworks shooting inside me.

I deserved to applaud every single one of my milestones, no matter how small they were.

After all, where was life, if not in the little things that made it wonderful? No matter how hard the rest seemed. Yes, the little things, details that could look insignificant from an outsider's point of view but deserved as much love and pride as big accomplishments.

Champagne. Yes, I'd celebrate my own success. On my own terms.

Work had never been so steady before. Great things would happen. I could feel it. A shift in the air. Or a good fortune.

I changed into a comfy sweater and a pair of worn-out jeans, added a coat of pink lipstick and some mascara.

Humming a song, I traipsed toward the kitchen counter to fetch my purse and car keys to fulfill my bubbly mission.

A loud pound resonated on the door.

My glee died, buried ten feet deep.

My cheerful heart turned to stone inside my chest.

A cold shiver ran from my head to my toes.

My pulse thrummed, heavy and strong.

I sensed him before he even opened his mouth.

Something dense clogged my airways.

My spine trembled at the idea of being used as a punching bag once more.

All the oxygen left my lungs, and my head spun.

My eyes brimmed with burning tears.

Why? Why couldn't he leave me alone today of all days? The hammering on the door intensified. It fractured more pieces of my heart. Little fragments I could never retrieve.

Robbie had a key. He usually let himself in, no matter the time. Maybe he had lost it. I hoped he had lost it. Perhaps if I pretended I wasn't here, he'd go away. He'd find another outlet for his anger—someone else who wasn't me.

Because I knew Robbie only came here if wrath bubbled inside him, and he had an urge to unwind. And only if he was wasted.

As if being drunk was a good enough excuse to beat me senseless. Like he couldn't bring himself to do it when he was sober.

Some part of him still cared for me. At least I hoped he did.

No matter what, his demons were bigger, faster, and

stronger, and they robbed him of everything that had once been good in him

Sober Robbie, even using hurtful words, only manhandled me. Sober Robbie didn't beat the shit out of me. Sober Robbie wasn't that much of a monster. Sober Robbie still possessed restraint. Sober Robbie was able to stop himself just before it was too late.

Drunk Robbie was unpredictable. Drunk Robbie relished hurting me. Drunk Robbie enjoyed the violence and the power he held over another human being.

Drunk Robbie stole all my innocence.

———

I shut my eyes, sealing the burning tears inside, refusing to let them out. Refusing to give my stepbrother any more control over my life. Over me.

I was stronger than what he credited me for.

Robbie's fist struck heavier on the door. My entire being trembled with each vibration as the sound rattled through me, deep in my core, shaking my very bones.

With my forehead pressed against the door, I struggled to catch a breath in. The tears escaped and burned trenches in my flesh.

"Devon, I…I know *youuu're* in there. Open up, *sisss*," he slurred, his voice sliced with anger. "I need *youuu*. You're all I've got left in this…in this life. Open the *dammmn* door. Don't force *meee* to break it from the hinges."

I pinched my lips together, crying silent tears.

Please go away. I'm having a great week. Don't mess it up. Please. Just leave. All I wished for was a celebration. And some champagne.

Why was I always the one dealing with this version of him? I hated this guy. And that guy hated me, even if he repeated I was his whole life while using my body as an outlet.

"*Devvvon*. Let. Me. In. I know *youuu're* in there. Your car is parked in front. And I can…I can feel you." He hiccupped. "*Stoppp* playing games."

Mrs. Glifford's voice joined his. "Ms. Devon, let your brother in. I don't want that man standing on my doorstep and disturbing my peace. Do you want me to call the cops?"

Sarcastic laughter bubbled out. As if the cops coming here could change a thing. They would probably force Robbie inside my apartment for all I knew. And tell me to care for him and be nice to his drunk ass. Yeah, it had happened before.

"*Devvvon*, it's my last warning. *Youuu* either let me in, or I'll let *myyyself* in."

Every cell in me shook. Another voice rose from the other side of the door. A man's voice this time. "Yeah, let the guy in. Just deal with your shit in private. No need to get the entire building to witness your squabble, for God's sake."

"Okay, that's it, I'm calling the cops," Mrs. Glifford said.

My hand wrapped around the doorknob, and with trembling fingers, I unlocked the latch.

My elderly neighbor gave me stinky eyes, her arms folded over her ample chest when my gaze landed on her. "It's about time." She waved her hands in the air and spun on her heels before retreating into the safety of her apartment. I wanted to implore her not to leave me alone with him, but I stood there on unsteady legs, unable to speak a word.

"Yeah, it-it's about *dammmn* time," Robbie echoed. He shoved me square in the chest with an open palm as he made his way inside. I stumbled backward, using the wall to regain my balance.

With a soft thud, I closed the door behind me, making sure not to lock it. In case I needed to run for my life. Or if someone walked by and heard the noises and flew to my rescue. Parts of me still had hope that it would happen. Someday.

With a jagged breath, I tried to steel my shoulders and relax at the same time.

This will be over in no time. Don't resist. Don't fight back. Try to talk some sense into him. It worked once. It can work again.

Don't push him. Agree with him. No smile. No sudden movement. No doing whatever could enrage him.

Mama, please protect me, I prayed in silence as Robbie paced the room.

My apartment wasn't big. Two bedrooms, a small bathroom, and a living room that also served as a dining area adjacent to a tiny kitchen. It had large windows letting lots of sunlight in, white walls reminding me of purity and calm, and maple hardwood floors.

Right now, it felt like a cage. Haunted by dark shadows.

And so small I was suffocating.

As if the walls were closing in on me. Squeezing the life out of me. Killing me in their own way.

My pulse throbbed in my ears. I couldn't swallow anymore, my throat dry and itchy. A tall glass of water would feel amazing right now, but I wouldn't dare to move and risk upsetting my stepbrother. Something resembling a chain coiled around my stomach, my heart, my lungs, tightening until pain seared through me.

Many emotions battled inside me. Voices in my head pleaded with me to leave. To run as fast and as far as I possibly could.

To disappear and never come back. To a place where

nobody could ever find me. Far from here. Far from everything I'd ever known.

"Why did *youuu* leave me in the hallway like a…like a fucking stray dog, *Devvvon*? You owe me respect, *sisss*. I've been taking care of your ass for *yeaaar*s, never asking anything in return. And this is *youuur* way of thanking me? By-by faking *youuu're* not home, hoping I'd go away? Is that all I'm… Is that all I'm worth to *youuu*? Because I think you haven't gotten the lesson *byyy* now." He padded closer, his breath now mingling with mine.

Everything inside me froze. Just a push and I'd break into countless pieces. I held my breath.

Robbie's finger almost touched my nose as he waggled it in my face, fury lacing every word coming out of his mouth. "*Youuu*. Belong. To. Me. We-we're family, and that's how family *workkks*. You…*youuu* need me as much as I…as I need you. And *youuu* do everything I say. All. The. Fucking. Time. I-I'm the boss of you. When will you understand that once *annnd* for all? Do you need *meee* to tattoo it on *youuur* forehead?" He let out a blood-freezing laugh. One that turned all my vital organs to ice. "The more I think *abouuut* it, the…the more branding *youuu* sounds like a good idea."

The fragile house of my hopes crumbled inside me.

Tears rushed to my eyes. I blinked—fast—and hoped Robbie hadn't noticed it. I didn't need to be lectured and taught again about how to be attentive to his crazy and delusional speeches. I already got that one once, and it had left me with a dislocated shoulder.

I locked my panic deep down and took a step back, putting some much-needed distance between us. Using an even and calm tone, I tried to reason with him. "Robbie. I'm sure you've had a hard day. I'm glad you came to me. If you wish, I could make you something to eat. And we could talk about it. You know I'm a good listener. We used to have long brother-and-sister discussions back in the day."

"*Fuuuck* that, *sisss*. I don't wanna talk," he screamed.

I blew out a quivering breath. Take two. I could disarm the bomb he had turned into. "We shouldn't yell because Mrs. Glifford next door will call the cops."

"*I'mmm* the fucking cops, *Devvvon*. Are you born stupid, or did *youuu* lose brain cells since the…since the last time I saw you?" He stepped closer. "Don't fucking ever tell *meee* what to do. Am I making myself clear? I'm the boss of *youuu*, sis. Don't ever forget that."

I swallowed. Hard. And nodded. "Yes. You are right. You're the boss," I said in a low, neutral voice, not letting any of my emotions seep through.

Robbie relaxed his stance, and some of the tension in his back seemed to vanish.

Feeling brave, I gave it another try. If I could just defuse his wrath, maybe I could reach the reasonable part of him before he decided to strike "Robbie, come sit. I'll get you something to drink. And then we can talk."

His head sprang up, and he glared at me with watery eyes. Was my brother crying? In all the years I'd known him, I'd never seen him cry. Not once. Not even when we were kids, or at our parents' funeral. "I-I'm tired of talking, *Devvvon*. I have…I have to blow off some steam. *Thaaat's* the only way I can relax. And get…and get through with *myyy* life. It's all messed up in-in my head. The voices..they won't shut up. Whatever I do, they…they nag at *meee*. Even in my sleep. Don't…don't resent me, *okaaay*? It has…it has nothing to do with *youuu*." He paused, as if to gather his thoughts. "You're my salvation, *Devvvon*. My…my safe place."

For a moment, I believed the real Robbie, the one I

looked up to growing up, had reappeared from the pits of hell. For a moment, he looked away, eyes vacant. When they met mine again, darkness claimed his face once more. The brother I knew had vanished, swallowed by the devil he'd become. In one swift movement, Robbie discarded his jacket on the sofa and rolled up his shirt sleeves to his elbows. I glanced at the door, searching for an escape route, already knowing my fate. But before I could move, he jumped in front of me, blocking the way out.

"Don't-don't even think *abouuut* running, *Devvvon*, or that will be the last time *youuu* see the light of the day."

Even his voice had turned satanic. Deprived of any goodness.

Every organ in my body hurt. And they hadn't even received penance yet.

I hid my hands in the sleeves of my green sweater—my favorite one—the moment Robbie's fingers gripped the fabric and he tugged me forward, my feet not touching the floor for a second or two.

He threw me on the hardwood surface, and my head took a hit. For a minute, dark spots danced in my vision, and I couldn't register the words leaving my stepbrother's mouth. A kick landed in my ribs, taking my breath away. And another one. Soon I came back to my senses and folded my arms over my face, trying to protect it from the hits. Robbie didn't have the same decency as his dad to spare everything above my neckline. He yelled at me, called me names, but I heard nothing. I lowered one arm to hold my ribs, and Robbie used that distraction to spit in my face.

Tears formed but stayed trapped in my eyes.

I barely caught my breath before I was hauled into the air and shoved against the wall, one strong hand encircling my throat and making it almost impossible for me to drag any oxygen in.

I lashed out with all my strength, but my kicks did nothing.

In a desperate attempt to get some help, I tried to cry. To scream. To beg. But Robbie's hard grip crushed my airways.

Just when I became lightheaded and thought I'd faint, he dropped me on the floor like a rag doll and slapped my face.

He pulled at my sweater, fisting the fabric until it ripped to drag me from the entryway to the living room, and I bumped my head on something hard in the wake.

A tingly sensation in my lower face told me my lips and jaw were beginning to swell.

More tears prickled my eyes, but none escaped their prison.

For a moment, I wished I could die. Then this would stop. Forever. Was it how my mother felt? The strongest part of me wanted to fight. To defeat the monster. To find a way out of this misery. To seek refuge elsewhere. Somewhere Robbie could never find me. Far from here.

But another part of me, the weak one, prayed this would be the last time. That I would never wake up from it and never have to relive another of his violent episodes ever again. That some god would hear and answer my plea.

I forced my brain to come back into the present.

Above me, my stepbrother insulted me—but I registered none of his words as he pressed his shoe into my already sore ribcage.

The survivor part of me kicked in.

The strongest part won the battle in my head.

I would fight. I would win this. And I would never let him hurt me ever again.

This had to stop. For good. I wouldn't be another victim.

I would beat the beast and emerge on the other side stronger, wiser. And braver.

My brain processed my new mission. If I survived this attack, it would be the last time Robbie assaulted me.

Like I'd seen the animals who sensed danger do in a documentary about wildlife and ignoring the aching throbs throughout my body, I lay on the floor as if Robbie had kicked the life out of me. Inert. All my focus was on keeping my breaths slow and superficial.

When I didn't react to his onslaught, he stepped back. I could feel the heat of his gaze on me. It burned my skin as if he'd used a scorching poker to brand me. Like that time he offered to tattoo his words on my forehead.

I begged my tears to resorb themselves and not betray me. Once more. Just one last time.

"Are *youuu* fucking dead, *sisss*?" Robbie slurred. "Oh God, *youuu're* even more useless than I…than I thought. What the *fuuuck*. Don't you dare die on me. *Youuu're* all I have to get through this…this darkness, *Devvvon*. The-the only one remaining. Everyone else has left *meee*. Don't you die, *okaaay*? Don't…please don't fucking leave me too. I-I just can't take it anymore. How will I… God, how will I survive without *youuu*?"

This time, there was no mistake. Robbie was crying. Weeping.

"My-my mom, Harry, *youuur* mom, my…my wife. They all abandoned *meee*. They…huh…they all loved you more than they…than they ever loved *meee*. Harry *nevvver* called me his precious child. Or…or the apple of his eyes. He favored *youuu*. Th-they all did. They saw *youuu* as a fucking saint. But no fucking saint got *fuckkked* by a guy in a…in a bar and played slut at a star-studded party. *Theyyy* were wrong. And like a fool, I-I protected *youuu*. For what? *Youuu* turned your back on me too. If you'd ever loved *meee*, you wouldn't have needed to flirt with ass…holes. You would have known I was…I was all you needed. That I loved *youuu*. I fucking did. But one day you'll-you'll leave me too. And I…I can't let it happen. So, don't die, *okaaay?* Do you hear me?" he hollered. "Do you hear me, *sisss?* You're not…you're not allowed to die. I'm the boss of *youuu*. I-I'll always be. And *youuu* won't ever get to leave me. That… that I promise you. *Youuu'll* never leave *meee*. Because I won't let you."

Pushing my emotions down as far as I could, I lay still, my body at a weird angle, my ribs hurting like hell, but doing my best not to show any signs of life.

My stepbrother threw something against the wall, and the sound of shattering glass startled me. Still, I didn't stir. I would never give him the pleasure to see me alive. No. If I did, he'd attack me again. This time, he would never stop. Until my last breath left me.

A shiver ran through me. My heart bled. Would it ever heal? Would I ever fully heal?

After seconds, minutes, or hours—I couldn't tell— Robbie grumbled something and let himself out, the door vibrating behind him as he left me for dead, not even bothering to see if I was still alive.

Chapter 9

"**D**evon? Is that you?" A fresh wave of acid made it to my mouth, and I swallowed hard to push it back down.

Without thinking further, I closed the gap between us and tipped her chin up with one finger.

"I-I'm sorry… I'm sorry to…to bother you," she said, sobs drowning her words.

Bruises covered her cheeks, and her lips and jaw were swollen. She looked nothing like the woman I'd met at that party a year ago, but more like a street fighter.

"Who did that to you? Talk to me."

My mother wasn't the only one who could sober me up with just a glance or a few words. Devon had that power too.

Adrenaline shot through me, and all the remnants of the alcohol marinating my organs disappeared. *Poof.* All gone.

"I…I can't…" Silent tears rolled down her battered cheeks. "I can't move. It-it hurts too bad."

"I'll call for help. Stay still," I said as I wrapped an arm around her heaving shoulders.

"*Nooo*." Her voice came out like the cry of a wounded animal. "No…no cops, okay? Please. No cops." She used the hem of her shirt to dry her soaked face.

"You sure? You're pretty banged up. You need medical attention."

"*Pleaaase*." She was pleading now, each word soaked in pain. "No cops. No one…no one can know I'm here."

I ran a hand through my hair, unable to decide what to do.

Devon's teary eyes locked on mine. I saw the despair in them. The distress. The pain. The fear.

"Fine. Okay. I'll help you in, though. You can't stay out here."

"I…I did it." I twisted toward her. What was she talking about? No way could she have beaten herself up. That made no sense. "I-I threw rocks at the lights. I didn't want… I couldn't risk anyone seeing me here. In case he —" She shook her head. "Never mind."

The lights. Oh. I'd forgotten about them.

With newfound energy and a clear mind, I unlocked the front door, switched on the entryway light, and stepped back outside to lift Devon, careful to be gentle. She weighed next to nothing in my arms. Once inside, I settled her on the L-shaped black couch and switched on a reading lamp in one corner of the living room.

The extent of her injuries looked far worse in the light.

A black eye, dry blood under her nostrils, a scratch on the side of her face, bruises on her cheeks and around her neck. Did someone strangle her? The idea sent cold chills down my back. Swelling distorted the bottom half of her face, and her mint-green sweater hung torn at the side.

Whoever did that to her was a dead man. If nobody else killed him first, I'd be the one doing the honor.

Rage flared from my pores. My fists curled at my sides.

I swallowed the fireball down my throat and sat next to her.

I inhaled, chasing some of my madness away—for her sake—and lowered my voice so I wouldn't scare her. "Listen to me. You need to report this to the police. You may have broken ribs or internal injuries. I'll go with you. I'll get Carter's security team, and they'll protect you. You can trust me."

Devon's red-rimmed eyes found mine, and she shook her head. Just a little, but enough for me to see it. "No. I… I'll be fine. It's not the first time. I-I just need a little time to heal."

A red-hot, scorching frenzy surged through my veins. I blinked, struggling to contain the wrath boiling inside me.

"He hurt you before?" She nodded. "Are you joking right now?" She shook her head. "Damn it." I sprang to my feet and began pacing the room, my fingers laced behind my neck, elbows flared out.

"Riley." Her voice was weak and shaky, missing the warmth I remembered from our first meeting. "I… Can I stay here? For a…huh…for a night? Or I-I can leave if you want. I…I didn't know where to go. And whom to trust. Robbie knows…he knows all my friends. I have no one…" Her voice broke, and something deep inside me shattered with it.

I stopped in my tracks and turned to her, wrestling the rage down—again, for her sake. "Why me? Why did you come here? Why now?" A ton of questions bounced around in my head. I deserved answers.

Devon's eyes filled with a fresh batch of tears. She looked like a little girl, her hands hidden in the sleeves of her torn sweater. She sniffled. "The-the night we met, you…made an impression on me. I knew from the start you had no evil in you. Remember how you reacted when that waitress spilled her tray on you? I could tell you were kind, honest, and good. You're not, huh, the only one able to read other people."

A little smile tugged the corner of her mouth, and I returned it.

Could she tell she'd been haunting every one of my nights since we met on that rooftop?

Squaring my shoulders, I asked the question burning on the tip of my tongue. "How did you find me? I never told you my last name or where I lived?"

Devon hung her head low and slouched back into the couch, her face twisting in pain. "This is so humiliating." She shut her eyes, fat tears hanging from her eyelashes.

A tug-of-war rose inside me. As much as I wanted to hold and care for her, I wanted to go out, find that motherfucker, and give him a taste of his own medicine.

Stuffing more of my ire away, I inched closer. "Tell me. It's okay." Was it, though? I never had strangers scouting my address before. I wasn't a celebrity by any means. Just the son of one and a manager to some. My personal life wasn't interesting in the public eyes, and I didn't even require bodyguards.

Devon spoke in a trembling voice. "I…I looked you up. Many times. Because I wanted to make amends. To-to explain myself. The reason I left that night—" A loud sob escaped. "I'm sorry. I sound like a psycho." She ran the back of her hand under her nose. "Riley, manager to Carter Hills. You…you weren't hard to trace down. When I figured out which neighborhood you lived in, I drove around whenever I had some free time, trying to catch sight of you.

"One day, it was late, and I saw you climb into your car. I promised myself I'd return and find the courage to come clean. But…but when that day came, I freaked out. I was scared you'd think I was a lunatic…a stalker…after I promised you I wasn't a groupie. I never drove through this neighborhood ever again. Until tonight."

My eyes widened at her admission. "You drove here? In this state?" I asked, gesturing to the length of her with my hand.

She shook her head. Her blonde curls were a mess. Blood-matted on one side and tangled and frayed like a bird's nest all around her head. "No. I…I walked. It took me…huh…hours to reach your street. Every step hurt, but I made sure not to leave a trace of where I was going. I even discarded my phone. In case he…he'd installed a tracking app I didn't know anything about, giving away my location." She sucked in a breath, wincing when she released it. "By the time I had stoned all the front porch lights, I-I fell asleep, too tired to stay awake to wait for you. I prayed you'd come home and that you weren't following Carter Hills or any of your other artists on the road." A lone tear streamed down her cheek, and she hurried to wipe it away with her sleeve. "I-I don't know what I would've done if you had been. I have nowhere… I have nowhere else to go. I'm so scared. And I can't… I just can't go through this again. He'll break me. Eventually, I won't be able to recover from this. I refuse to give him that much power over me. He-he'll have my soul."

"Hey, it's okay. I'm here. I'm not going anywhere. You can trust me." I kneeled in front of her and with care, held her shaking cold hands between mine. "But why? Why didn't you come here sooner if he's hit you so many times this past year?"

She bent her head down. "I was ashamed. I couldn't let you see me like that…so broken. All I wished was for you to remember me the same way I looked that night. The woman you felt a deep connection with." She shook her head and offered me a speck of a smile. "I know how silly it sounds now. I just… I thought…"

"Devon, it's okay. You are here now. He won't find you. You can cry. And you can stay here. We'll figure it out. I promise."

I brushed her hair back gently with my fingers as she shed more tears. Leaning forward, she buried herself in my arms. At first, I stood frozen, unsure how to comfort her without causing more pain. But after a moment, I wrapped my arms around her trembling body, hoping to plant seeds of hope in her as she let herself be vulnerable with me.

Once the tremors racking her body subsided, I held out my hand and rose to my feet. "Come on, let's get you cleaned up."

Chapter 10
Riley

Devon's trust in me, conveyed through the gentle touch of her palm, shot straight through my heart as we made our way to my bedroom. I rummaged through my closet and fetched a pair of gray sweatpants and a Carter Hills Band vintage T-shirt. I motioned to the chair in the corner by the window. "Wait here. I'll fill the bathtub." I put the folded pile of clothes on the bed. "You change into these. I can get you a new wardrobe by tomorrow morning if you give me your size."

She avoided my gaze and nervously fidgeted with her fingers in her lap. "No. It's okay. You don't need to go through that much trouble for me. Just a place to sleep for the night is more than enough. I-I'll come up with a plan tomorrow. Don't worry about me."

I stepped forward but kept a distance between our bodies. "No. You're staying here for as many nights as you need to. You'll be safe. I'll make sure of it. This house has the latest security system. Will add more if necessary."

Her voice carried a note of complaint. "That's what he always says…" She snorted. "That he's doing this to keep me from being harmed. Whatever it means."

I blinked. Hard. My own eyes burned with unshed tears.

"Wait. No. I'll never hurt you. I swear."

Devon hung her head lower. "I…I know."

"Getting you a new wardrobe is the least I can do. You need a fresh start, and I'm offering you one. Just say yes and let me be there for you."

She finally lifted her gaze to meet mine, her eyes searching for the truth behind my words. We exchanged promises only our souls could comprehend right now.

More tears welled up in Devon's eyes, making them appear larger. The exhaustion and gratitude shining in them humbled me.

If she weren't all banged up, would she let me hold her? Comfort her heart the way it needed?

She brought a hand to her face to rub off her tears but the motion made her wince.

I flinched inside at the sight of her injuries. I stepped closer and used my thumb to dry the stream gently. Something woke up inside me. A need to protect her. Even with my own life. With careful fingers, I pushed the wild tendrils of her hair away from her face, making sure she had no wounds requiring immediate attention.

Most of them were bruises.

And the scratch on her face looked superficial. No stitches needed.

My breath hitched, the internal tug-of-war resuming. Not getting her other injuries checked felt wrong. It didn't sit well with me. "You sure you don't wanna go see a doctor? Maybe I can find one who makes house calls."

"No. I know what a broken face feels like. And this? This isn't it. I can tell."

My stomach knotted. She could tell what a broken face felt like? What was wrong with this world? Anyway, how could someone beat another person senseless? Who could be cruel enough to inflict such wounds on another human being?

Chunks of my heart plummeted down my chest, and bile rose in my throat.

I sucked in some air, not willing to let the woman in front of me see how much I was affected.

The vulnerability in her eyes broke me some more. With the gentlest touch, I curled my hand around the back of her neck and drew her close. She deserved to be comforted. Or maybe it was me who craved comfort, my heart and head unable to grasp the weight of her tragedy.

My thoughts raced in my head. Dizziness troubled my senses.

I leaned back, fighting my emotions and begging them to stay put."Gimme a few minutes. I'll fill the bathtub and come back to get you." I inhaled. "Devon, before we do that, would you allow me to take pictures of your wounds? It will be used as evidence if you decide to go to the cops... or press charges."

Her breath caught as tears sprang to her eyes. Having her abuse photographed would be the most humiliating thing for her. My heart bled at her pain. How I wished I could whisk her away from it all and heal her. But almost before my eyes, I saw strength push the embarrassment aside. And she nodded.

I spoke in a low voice. "I promise to be careful." As I raised my phone, I vowed justice for her.

"It's…it's okay. I know you will."

My eyes recorded each hit, each punch, the ache inside me deepening into a dark abyss at the horrors she had faced today. I felt deep respect for her courage and the trust she showed me. She was truly inspiring.

After the ordeal, I left her sitting on the bed while I ran a bath. The entire time I was in the bathroom, I cursed under my breath. I had to find that guy. There was no way I could live with myself if I didn't. I'd get Taylor—Carter's chief of security—on it first thing tomorrow morning. We'd find that coward who hurt women like it was a side hustle. He didn't deserve to be called a man.

Fucking psycho.

Leaning over the sink, I splashed cold water on my face. I looked like shit. For the last hour, I'd forgotten about my own state of intoxication. My hair was a mess, my eyes bloodshot, and my stubble two days too long. Devon and I made quite a pair. I stifled a bitter chuckle.

My thoughts were spinning way too fast for my liking. How was I supposed to act around her? What was I supposed to do? After all, I was born with a silver spoon in my mouth and had never faced that kind of violence first-hand. Never before in my life had I met a woman who'd been used as a punching bag. This was all new to me. I had no reference point whatsoever in domestic violence situations.

I snapped back to the present when the bathroom door opened, and Devon slid through the opening. "Can I come in? I don't want to be alone." I nodded. "And also, you'll have to help me out of these clothes because my ribs hurt like hell."

I swallowed the ball of anger bobbing in my throat, feeling on the verge of exploding inside. Once air made it back to my brain, I relaxed my stance a little.

I'd witnessed Carter's panic attacks before, and I refused to go there. Of the two of us, he had always been the emotional one, and I, the pragmatic one. This wouldn't change. Not tonight. I wouldn't yield to my conflicted emotions.

"Here. Take these," I said, offering Devon two painkillers and a glass of water. "It's not much, but it should help with the pain… I hope."

"Thanks." She took the pills with a gulp of water, then turned so her back was to me. I helped her out of her torn sweater, its fabric stained with what looked like blood…her blood.

She shivered under the pads of my fingers. I shivered too.

We hadn't seen each other in a year—and only for a night—and still, the touch of her was intoxicating enough to send waves of heat through me.

And somehow it felt like we had known each other for far longer.

"Need help with your jeans too?"

She bobbed her head, keeping it hanging low. I didn't want her to feel humiliated, so I closed my eyes as I pushed her pants down her legs, making sure her panties stayed on.

"Thanks," she whispered.

I helped her into the bubble bath, and once she settled in and the bubbles covered her chest, I unclasped her bra. Sitting with her legs folded, she slipped off her underwear and put them on the edge of the bathtub.

"I'll be outside. Tell me if you need anything"—I clenched the doorknob hard enough to murder it—"unless you want me to wash your hair." My heart cracked in my chest as I looked at her battered form again. I couldn't move, couldn't walk away, as if my absence alone could endanger her.

Breathe, Riley, she's fine. She can't get hurt anymore.

Devon's gaze met mine, and we fixed on each other for a long beat. "I'd like that. Only if I'm not a burden."

"Nah. I'm the one who offered, remember?"

A small smile appeared on her split lips. The ones I'd wanted to feast on so badly that night. Her smile, even as tiny as it was, glued back a loose piece of my heart.

I gathered the shower essentials—I only had men's shampoo and soap, but I was sure Devon wouldn't mind—and a towel to wrap her hair afterward.

Relief washed through me when I saw the blood matting her hair came from the cut on her cheek, not a deeper wound. A few times, Devon's breath hitched as I gently massaged her scalp. A yelp of pain left her mouth, and it shattered my heart. It fired my blood. Nobody should go through this kind of violence. I just hoped that my gentle touch would help ease her pain and the effects of the abuse she'd been through. That I could somehow help heal her wounds and ease the memory of the trauma.

Even with the face of a boxer who had just lost a world championship, she still looked gorgeous to me. Just as I'd remembered her from that night in her red dress. Long neck. High cheekbones. Mesmerizing eyes.

With a washcloth and warm water, I cleaned the wounds on her face with as much care as I could muster, our eyes never breaking contact.

Thirty minutes later, we lay on our sides, facing each other on my bed. "You're sure you want to sleep in here? With me? I can move into a guest room."

"No. Please, stay. I'm…I'm scared. I know it's silly. Robbie can't get to me here. But…huh…I don't want to be alone. Do you mind? I feel like I'm intruding on your life—"

"You're not. I'm honored you came to me. Wake me up if you need anything. Even if it's only to talk, okay?"

"Thanks, Riley." Devon extended her hand until she knitted her shaky fingers through mine.

I watched her for hours as her breathing slowed and sleep finally claimed her.

Even hours later, my heart still ached for the beating she'd suffered.

I pulled the blanket over her shoulders and inched closer, praying my presence would be enough to chase away the bad guys in her nightmares.

Devon's grip on my hand never wavered, and I fell asleep as we both held on to each other.

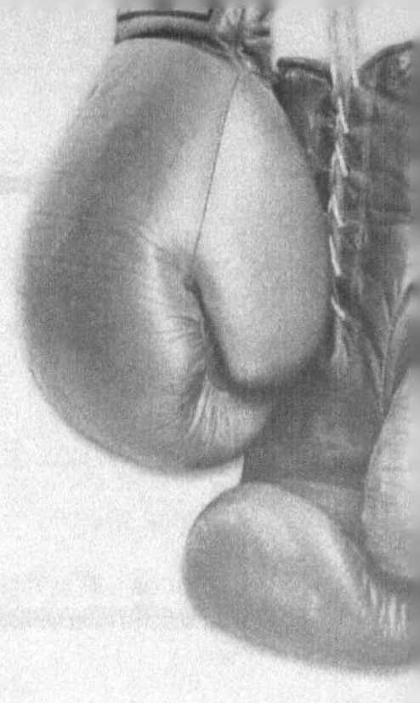

Chapter 11
Devon

I woke with a start, my heart racing and my thoughts spinning. For a moment, I couldn't remember where I was. Pain radiated along my jaw, and I dabbed at my swollen lower lip with a fingertip. Oh yes, the attack. Robbie leaving me for dead on my apartment floor. Running away and leaving everything I owned behind. Collapsing on Riley's front porch where he found me afterward. The way he took care of me, making sure I was safe after I'd opened up to him a little about what had happened.

The memories all felt both distant and painfully recent at once. I felt like I had aged ten years since escaping my home earlier.

In the darkness, I heard the soft breathing of the man lying beside me. Our fingers were still intertwined. The night replayed in my mind—little details that confirmed I had been right that night when I had assumed Riley Burns was a good man.

Earlier, on our way to his bedroom after he had offered to help me clean up, we passed a few rooms. His bedroom was spacious, even boasting an en-suite bathroom. "We'll use my room since it has a bathtub," he had said. After I reluctantly agreed for him to record my injuries—because Riley was right, they could be useful if I decided to bring my stepbrother to justice—my host left me in the low-lit bedroom all by myself to fill the tub. I hugged my stomach with my arms, trying to bring my body some much-needed comfort, doing my best to avoid crushing my sore midriff.

Every inch of me suffered the aftermath of Robbie's onslaught. Even my vertebrae screamed in pain. They were still screaming hours later.

Humiliation swirled inside me at the idea of having a stranger photograph the extent of the beating I had endured. But no matter how uncomfortable it felt to have an object pointed at me, memorizing each wound, knowing those proofs wouldn't be buried by Robbie this time, gave me the strength to go through with it. My stepbrother wouldn't get a chance to erase the evidence with threats or blackmail now. I could control the narrative and wouldn't be subject to agreeing with his twisted retelling of the events if I sought medical help or found a way to bring him down for the abuse he had put me through.

From where I sat on his bed, I heard Riley—the most selfless man I'd ever met, now I was sure of it—muttering something from the bathroom.

Shivers coursed through me as memories of the night flashed back in my mind.

I remembered pushing myself to my feet, scanning the space around me, so foreign, yet somehow comforting all at once. A king-sized bed with a dark comforter and a bunch of decorative pillows, a dark blue upholstered wingback chair in a corner, a fluffy matching-colored rug at the end of the bed. On each side, there was a dark wooden night-stand, matching the headboard.

White walls. Straight lines. A few white accents.

The room looked masculine, modern-chic, and rustic all at once.

Loneliness fell over me like a thick curtain, and my heart sped up.

I was in a stranger's bedroom. By myself. And for some reason, I still suspected Robbie would show up and steal me away. Away from salvation. Away from freedom.

I heard the water running, and before my mind caught up with my feet, I reached the bathroom threshold and pushed the door ajar.

"Can I come in? I don't want to be alone."

Riley nodded, his face a mask of worry.

I inhaled some courage to speak the next words. "And also, you'll have to help me out of these clothes because my ribs hurt like hell."

Admitting it out loud sent moisture to my eyes. I wasn't the type of woman to ask for help. My mother had died a decade ago, and I'd learned to be self-sufficient at a young age. Until Robbie tried to steal my free will and independence by watching my every move with his friends, using me to unwind every time his stress levels reached new highs.

I accepted the painkillers Riley offered and swallowed them with a painful sip. Over-the-counter medication was my only ally, numbing some of the pain since a trip to the clinic wasn't an option.

With a gentleness I hadn't witnessed since I was a little

girl, he peeled the sweater over my head. Then he moved in front of me, closed his eyes, and slid my jeans down my legs before helping me into the bathtub.

I eased down, relishing the warm, bubbly water. The lavender scent filled my nostrils, and some tension left my upper back.

By the door, he froze. I met his gaze, and we just stared at each other for a long moment. Why was this man so kind to me? Why did he agree to tend to me without asking anything in return? His irises glistened, and I wondered if it was from sadness—or fury.

Minutes later, I grimaced as his fingers massaged my scalp. Even if it sent a rush of pain through me, the gesture also sent flutters to my broken heart.

Yes, not all men were born equal.

And Riley Burns was a special kind of man.

After changing into the clothes he lent me, I followed him back to his bedroom, where he helped me ease under the covers as every movement drew a groan of pain from me. I gently turned onto my side to relieve the pressure on my sensitive ribs.

He studied my features for a moment before offering to sleep in the guest room.

The idea of being alone sent an earthquake through my heart, shaking its foundation to its core.

My voice trembled on its way out as I pleaded for him to stay—to not leave me alone in the dark. And for once, in a very long time, I knew I could sleep peacefully. Safely.

Without overthinking it, I intertwined my fingers with his, hoping he wouldn't pull away. I knew it made no sense to ask him to sleep in the same bed as me, but everything inside me felt flimsy and precarious. I wasn't sure I could sleep on my own without having a breakdown or a panic attack.

Tonight's beating had been the worst I'd ever endured. I was surprised the damage wasn't more extensive. There had been times in the past when I'd lain on the floor for hours, unable to move a bone.

And one time, I'd had such a bad concussion the room spun afterward, and I fainted in my vomit.

Perhaps this time had been all about survival.

Perhaps it would have been deadly if I hadn't faked being unconscious.

I still had no idea how I'd walked the seven-point-nine miles from my apartment to Riley's place on legs that shook with every step. In my head, I'd been so focused on getting there without being spotted that I waited until dark to make my escape. I'd wanted to change beforehand, but since I couldn't lift my arms, I'd forfeited the idea. I brought nothing along, afraid I wouldn't make it if I carried a bag because my body felt too weak to support the weight.

Many times on my way here, I thought about giving up, but I craved freedom. I craved control of my life again. And that would never happen if I didn't find a way out of Robbie's reach. So I walked until I couldn't stand upright. And then walked some more.

Emotions bubbled up inside me at the memory of my eyes landing on the street sign, and how I'd burst into tears as if a heavy weight had been lifted from my shoulders.

I had made it.

Maybe now I could move on with my life.

Maybe I could find help, change my name if needed, request protection… And finally leave the city I loved so much.

The clock on the bedside table read almost five in the morning. I had to stop fighting sleep and surrender myself once more. My body was exhausted. My mind shattered. I had nothing left to give.

If I wanted to heal, I needed the rest.

Scooting closer to the man beside me, I closed my eyes, never letting go of his hand.

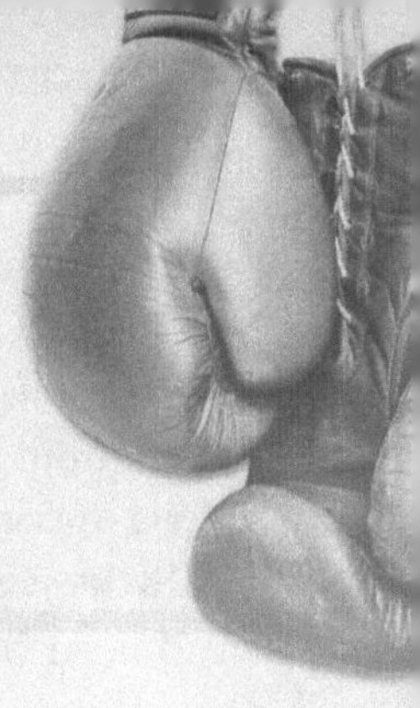

Chapter 12
Riley

The next morning, I woke up early, with a woman I didn't remember inviting home nestled against me, her front pressed to mine, her face buried in my chest, and my arms around her waist. Then my brain rebooted, and memories of last night surfaced.

Devon.

How could I forget?

I propped myself up on one elbow and rested my gaze on her.

She looked peaceful in her sleep. The swelling on her cheekbones had lessened a little, but the bruises had darkened over the last few hours, now a deep indigo edging toward black.

I fastened the blanket around her, careful not to wake her up.

More pieces of my heart cracked in my chest at the sight of such a beautiful woman all banged up.

Her blonde hair surrounded her head, a contrasting halo to my black Egyptian cotton sheets.

In a slow motion, I eased my arm from around her, shifted from under the covers, rose from the bed, and tiptoed out of my bedroom to make a few calls.

Taylor, Carter's bodyguard, had lots of contacts in the city. I needed to talk to him first and see what information about that Robbie guy he could gather.

After we hung up, I dialed Juniper, my assistant, and asked her to get clothes delivered here as soon as possible. I trusted her. She asked no questions, and I was quietly grateful for her discretion.

Sitting in my office, I called Dr. Diaz, a therapist who had helped Carter deal with his panic attacks after his world exploded a few years ago. He was now our devoted therapist on speed-dial whenever one of us required psychological help.

"Hello, Mr. Burns. It's been quite some time. How can I help you?"

I explained to him what I knew about Devon's situation so far. I lacked details but still could give him a description of what happened since she first appeared on my front porch.

"Listen, Riley," Dr. Diaz said, "that woman, she needs help. But you can't force her to get any if she doesn't want to or isn't ready. I'll tell you what you can do, though. Listen. Don't judge. Be there for her. Offer her a shoulder to cry on, or a safe space where she feels secure enough to heal and share what she went through…if and when she's ready."

"Should I push for her to see a doctor? To see you?"

"No. Only she can make that decision. From what you said, it isn't the first time that man has beaten her. And she seems afraid to go to the authorities. Maybe she's right to be cautious, maybe not. But follow her lead. If she trusts you—which I assume she does, since she came to you—she'll open up when she's ready. At her own pace. Just make sure she knows she has access to resources if she changes her mind."

I scratched my nape. Annoyance simmered inside me. Dr. Diaz's words didn't please me, but deep inside, I knew they made sense.

I sighed. "Thanks. I'll keep that in mind."

He added, "You're doing great, Riley. Don't be so hard on yourself. That woman is lucky to have you in her corner. Follow your instincts. From what I've learned about you over the years, they're usually on point."

I exhaled. "Thank you, doc. I'll keep in touch."

"Whenever you need, son."

We hung up, and I returned to my bedroom to watch Devon from the doorway as she slept, wondering what to do next.

What could I do to support her?

Dr. Diaz's words replayed in my head. *Listen. Don't judge. And be there for her. Follow your instincts.*

What would happen to her?

Something deep in me had woken up last night. I wanted to care for her. To make sure she was okay. And that nobody could harm her anymore.

My desire to be around her was as powerful as the first time we met. Only, this time, it had nothing to do with lust, but everything to do with concern and protection.

Once I was sure she was safe and sound, I made a few more calls and canceled all my engagements for the weekend—an album launch party and a golf tournament. Only Devon mattered.

Chapter 13

Devon

When I woke up, I scanned the room around me. Panic settled in my core, but soon memories of last night flew in.

I had no idea what time it was, but by the light coming from the hallway, I knew it must have been late morning.

I squirmed on the mattress, and flashes of pain threatened to tear my body into pieces. A loud pounding resonated through my skull. Every inch of my skin tingled with an ache coming from deep inside me. My lips and jaw were numb.

I moved my hand up to feel the scratch on my cheek, and stifled a gasp of pain when my fingertip connected with the scraped skin.

With a weak arm, I pushed myself to a sitting position and noticed the painkillers and glass of water by the bed.

Riley.

A soft smile peeked on my lips.

After I tied my messy hair in a loose braid and adjusted my borrowed clothes, I aimed for the kitchen, my steps weary and small, doing my best not to make any abrupt movement.

Midway, I felt dizzy and had to steady myself against the wall until the waves of nausea passed.

When I reached the kitchen, Riley was cooking, and the smell told me he was making pancakes.

His kitchen had high planked ceilings, teal cupboards, stainless steel appliances, and a huge island with a wooden butcher-block countertop. It had a craftsman meet farmhouse and vintage vibe. And it suited him. Nothing too extravagant.

I watched him, humming a song, looking happy, dressed in sweats and bare feet, moving around with ease.

He swiveled, a turner in his hand, and our eyes locked.

A warm smile stretched his lips. "Hey you," he greeted, padding forward. "How did you sleep?"

I returned his smile, my lips cracking where they were split. "Like a rock. I just woke up once. What time is it?"

"Almost noon. You might have suffered a concussion, and I didn't notice last night. In fifteen minutes, I would have come to check on you… Just in case." I bowed my head as his worried eyes scanned my face. "Coffee? I'm making pancakes."

"Yes, please." Coffee—my slice of nirvana.

Riley offered me a mug and led me to a stool by the island.

"Thank you. For everything. I'll get out of here later." I tried to hide my weariness and the constant throb pulsing through every wounded inch of my body.

The man turned to face me, his smile dissolving completely. "No." He inched closer. "Devon, you don't have to leave. You said it yourself last night. You have nowhere to go. You're safe as long as you're in my home. There's no way that man will think to look for you here. Why don't you stay for now and come up with realistic options before making a hasty decision? You need to be someplace where you can heal without the risk of bumping into him. Give yourself some time. Unless you prefer I drive you to a women's shelter."

A surge of trepidation swirled in my stomach. I shook my head, noticing how stiff my neck was. "No. Please. Don't drive me to a shelter. I-I did once… Robbie is… He is a police officer. He knows people. He…he can find me there. He can find me almost everywhere."

A weight grew in my chest, suffocating me as it pressed against my lungs. My body trembled at the memory of the last time I tried to escape my stepbrother, only to be treated as if *he* were the innocent victim, always worrying for his brainless always-running-away little sister.

Riley squeezed my hand. "I won't. It's settled. You stay here. For as long as you need. And I'll help you. I promise you'll never have to be that man's punching bag ever again. You have my word."

I blinked tears. "Why? How? You don't have—"

He raised his hands between us. "I insist. Now you gotta eat something. Then we'll hang out if you feel like it, or you can go rest if you prefer. Whatever you choose, I'm not leaving you by yourself."

I tried to argue, but no words came out.

In all honesty, if Riley had asked me to go, I had no idea where I would have gone. I let out a sigh, putting my ego to rest, and accepted the strawberry pancake he offered me.

My favorite. How did he know?

The sweet scent and the sight of the juicy red fruits wrapped my heart in a thick coat of balm.

"I'd like to hang out with you if your offer still stands," I said, once I was done. "But nothing too physical or intellectual."

"You know what? It's been years since I relaxed for an entire day. Let's watch something and you can nap if you're tired. Deal?" I nodded. "Great. Let me get us blankets and snacks, and we'll be good to go."

Riley placed an ice pack before me on the countertop with a nod, leaving me to care for my bruises.

Chapter 14
Riley

Devon stood in the kitchen, watching me with apprehension and softness in her eyes. Her face was a map of bluish-black bruises, each one a sour reminder of what she had gone through during all these years. A mixture of pain and anger twisted my insides, creating a new surge of hatred for the man who inflicted such physical abuse on a woman. Fishing deep inside me to avoid scowling, I brought a neutral expression onto my face. Even with her flesh all smashed up, she still looked stunning. I firmed my back and stepped up to her, making sure to leave a comfortable space between us. The last thing I wanted was to scare her. I could offer shelter. And protection. And everything she needed to feel safe. If she wanted them…from me.

We ate in comfortable silence. As if we'd done it in the past and words were superfluous.

On a mission to offer her a breather, I exited the

kitchen with reluctant steps. Many questions swam in my head, but I couldn't rush them out. I would give her time to get to know me first, to trust me, before asking any of them.

Since I hadn't heard back from Taylor, I checked my phone to make sure I hadn't missed a call.

My gaze landed on Devon's discarded clothes in the bathroom, and I inhaled sharply and closed my eyes when images of last night rushed back to my mind.

My heart trembled at the memories of panic and terror clouding her eyes.

When I found her lying on my doorstep, death seemed close to taking her, trying to make her give up. But she kept fighting and refused to surrender. I was thankful she trusted me enough to ask for help. Devon was barely holding on, but she stayed strong—for me—and didn't give up. I was glad she kept fighting.

Last night, I struggled to hold back the urge to take away her pain and help heal her scars, even the ones you couldn't see but ran deep inside her. I was afraid to touch her fragile cheeks, worried I might hurt her. How could anyone mar such a gentle soul?

All I wanted was to kiss her forehead and promise her my unconditional support. To hug her against my heart and reassure her.

I wanted to fight her battles for her, but I knew she'd only accept help if I fought alongside her—helping her face her problems head-on.

Over the past year, Devon had become my world without even realizing it, even if I was just a small part of hers. And even if she never felt the same way, I knew I'd always hold on to the time we spent together. Still, I'd do everything I could to show her how much she meant to me

—that I could be the one to make her happy. If she'd let me.

Moisture rose at the back of my eyes, and a cold chill ran along my spine as I picked her bloody, torn clothes and put it in a paper bag as evidence if needed. She deserved her day of justice. And the bastard to be locked up forever, the key forgotten.

"Ready for that TV marathon?" I asked after I made popcorn and brought all our cocooning necessities to the living room.

"Absolutely."

We exchanged tight-lipped smiles while we took our place on opposite sides of the couch. Devon spread the blanket over her, and I handed her a pillow to support her arm.

For the longest time, I'd dreamed of finding her. But now that she'd found me, I had no idea what to do or say. In all the scenarios I'd imagined after she disappeared that night, her real story turned out far more horrifying than anything I could've anticipated—darker than any nightmare I'd ever known.

The pit of burning fury in my stomach seared each time my gaze found hers, but her smile, genuine and humble, tamed the flames, and I forgot all about avenging her, choosing to look out for her instead.

I shifted in my seat, wanting to hold her close, but I knew it would be too much, too soon. For now, having her in my home, spending time together, getting to know her, had to be enough.

I'd make sure nobody and nothing bad would get to her without going through me first.

Playing house, we binge-watched silly reality shows—something I hardly ever did, my schedule always too full to indulge in some me-time. Devon's clear laughter permeated the room, reminding me of the night we first met.

Someone rang the doorbell. The air froze around us, heavy with the stench of fear.

At the sound of the first peal, Devon startled, hugging herself with her arms as panic flickered in her eyes, and tension made her body go rigid. All the color drained from her face, making the bruises and cuts stand out even more. She folded her knees and curled tightly over herself, barely breathing. The hair on my arms stood on end, and my pulse quickened at the sight. She looked like a woman bracing to shield her body from punches and kicks. I couldn't breathe. A sinking realization hit me. This was what happened every time someone rang her doorbell. She knew the person would come in and unleash their anger on her.

My heart sunk low in my chest. My soul withered and died, and my respect for her touched sky high. Ohmygod, she had gone through so much. I wondered how she could even still be alive. Or how she could offer me small smiles every now and then when her world had been so dark for so long. That moment hit me like a thunderclap. I'd been living in my seemingly perfect little world for far too long, blind to all the devils lurking out there.

The doorbell rang again.

All my senses heightened, and I jumped to my feet, ready to send away whoever stood on the other side of the door.

"Wait here," I said, balling my hands into fists, not backing down from a fight if it all came down to it.

I stood tall, puffed out my chest to project confidence, and yanked the door open, holding my breath.

Juniper stood there, bags in her arms.

I emptied my lungs as relief washed through me. My

heart rate normalized. I worked hard to school my expression and project a casual vibe. Now I understood what Devon went through as I hadn't even realized how on edge I was until my assistant stood inches away from me. I scratched the side of my head as I glanced at her. "June? Huh…did you go…did you go shopping?"

She offered me a victorious smile. "I heard the emergency in your voice when you called this morning. I wouldn't have let anyone else do you the favor. I picked every piece myself. Got a bit of everything. Even a cute dress…just in case. And toiletries. A little makeup. Just some girls' stuff, you know." She gave me a slow once-over, studying my expression with furrowed brows. "I'm not gonna ask questions, though. All I'll say is that if you need my help with anything, call me. I'll drive the getaway car if that's what you need. All you gotta do is ask."

I nodded. "Thanks, June. I owe you one. You have no idea how happy I am it's you at the door right now."

"You okay? Should I worry? Were you waiting for someone else?"

I shook my head. "Nah. Everything is under control. Thank you for your help."

She winked at me and dropped a kiss on my cheek. "She must be a special someone."

I nodded while she handed me the bags before walking back to her car.

She pulled out the driveway, and I waved at her, breathing out every remnant of tension swirling inside me.

I was really ready to punch the jerk if he had been the one ringing the doorbell. I hadn't gone into a fight since I was like ten, but with adrenaline running high in my bloodstream, I would have kicked his ass. Big time. Yeah, he wouldn't have seen it coming. If only I knew what he looked like.

On lighter feet, I returned to the living room, but there was no sign of Devon anywhere. Did she go to the bathroom? Steel coiled around my stomach. No. She was hiding. I could sense it. The thickness in the air. The wings of terror floating in each room.

"Devon?" I called out. "Are you all right? It's just me."

A soft cry pierced my heart.

I neared my bedroom and pressed my forehead to the door. "It's okay. It's safe… You're safe." I bet the lump in my throat was the reason my voice was so shaky.

"Who was it?" she inquired from inside.

"My assistant, June. Can I come in? I promise there's no one else here. She…huh…she brought you stuff."

Sniffles and a whispered "Yes" came from the other side of the door.

With a careful gesture, I pushed it open, slowly, inch by inch.

The sight of Devon curled into a ball in the wingback chair, her arms circling her folded legs, tears streaming down her face broke me all over again.

I stepped inside the room, the light coming from the window illuminating her features.

"Would you like to have a look? June brought you clothes…amongst other things."

A mask of apprehension appeared on Devon's vulnerable face. "You told people about me being here? Riley, you…you shouldn't have done that. I-I'm not safe anymore. Robbie has contacts everywhere. It'll reach his ears." Her body shuddered, and I dashed to her side and stroked her back, wishing I could steal all her pain and fears away.

She flinched at first, then relaxed, scooted closer to me, allowing me to comfort her. She sucked in some air in halting gasps, and my heart fractured in my chest. My lips found the crown of her head on their own, and I laid a kiss there.

"Hey, I said nothing to June. Besides, she works with country music superstars for a living. She's used to keeping everything she sees or hears to herself. Don't worry. And no, I didn't tell her about you. I promise. She probably thinks I'm hiding a one-night stand or something. Anyway, it's none of her business... Your secret is safe with me." I cleared my throat and lowered my voice. "I need to know something, though." I breathed in and closed my eyes, images I preferred not to think about making their way to my mind. I huffed and braced myself for the truth. "Is Robbie...well...is he your husband?"

Devon stiffened in my embrace. After a few seconds, she shook her head.

"No. *No, no, no.* Robbie is actually my...my stepbrother. And he just likes to hit me. For, huh, no reason."

Okay, one less thing to worry about.

"He likes to hit me the same way his dad hit my mother in all their years of marriage. When I was ten, Robbie installed a lock on my bedroom door just in case. And told me to hide in there every time his dad was in one of his raging episodes...too many to count by then. One day, I thought I'd get my mom out of there, and we would be safe again. I imagined I'd bring Robbie along because he didn't deserve to be used as a punching bag either. Then our parents died in a car crash... From that day, Robbie became my legal guardian until I turned eighteen... Six years ago. Back then, we were fine. He had always been overprotective of me but had never hurt me. We-we got along great. Three years ago, something changed. His...his wife divorced him and ran away soon after. One night, he went crazy when he caught me in a bar with a guy I liked...a lot...after he'd ordered me to stay at home instead of going out with my friends. He acted like I was a teen and not a grown woman. It drove him nuts, and that's when…that's when he started using me as his personal anger-target.

"Robbie is a police officer and a very talented actor and manipulator… I'd even call him a sociopath. I don't have any leverage to get him arrested. He has friends in high places. I pressed charges twice, ran away three times, and all those times the beatings only worsened afterward. He said I had to be taught a valuable lesson… To never turn my back on him…since we're, huh, family. Anyway, nobody believed me when I said he did that to me. Robbie is considered some sort of hero because he saved a kid in a supermarket robbery a while back. People love him. They respect him. He plays the game of the upstanding citizen and devoted police officer perfectly." Her throat worked as she spoke the last few words. "So now, I keep the beatings to myself."

She cocked her head to the side and inhaled, fists resting in her lap, her back straight. I could almost see the tension radiating off her.

She breathed in again, and this time, she gazed down as the words slipped from her lips, doing her best to avoid my eyes.

"Yesterday, he came to my place after his shift, drunk as usual, and started insulting me through the door. I faked not being home—" She stopped and clasped her hands together, then continued. "My neighbors complained about the noise, and I let him in, not knowing what else to do. The last thing I needed was to get evicted on top of everything else. Anyway, I tried to talk him out of hurting me but failed. When I suggested we discuss what was bugging him, he attacked me, then choked me, and dragged me around. When I collapsed to the floor, he kicked me. I had to fake being unconscious, so he'd leave faster. It-it worked. After he left, I devised a plan and made my escape at sunset. I can't go to…huh…any of my friends. He knows them all." Tears glistened in Devon's eyes, bluer today in the daylight.

A mass of pain and anger took residence in my chest, crushing all my organs. Every time she opened up to me, her story only grew darker with each new detail. I inhaled and pushed my uneasiness aside, determined to stay strong for the woman who'd been living in hell far too long and needed my strength now.

"Devon, this is terrible. I'm sorry I asked. You should press charges. I'll come with you."

She ignored my words and kept talking. "That night, last year…at the party"—she bowed her head and fidgeted with her fingers—"Robbie showed up after he ambushed my friend and forced her to tell him where I was. He shoved her around and broke her wrist. She tried to call me, to warn me, but I didn't bring my phone in case he could track it. Robbie probably played the nice cop card to get past security. It worked. It always does. Anyway, he found me…again. He doesn't want me to have a life outside of him. I'm lucky I work from home as a free-lancer, because too often, I wouldn't be able to show up in public. Banged-up faces tend to attract unwanted attention."

A wave of molten fury woke inside me, demanding the right to decimate everyone in its path. I wanted to kill that bastard with my bare hands. Dark spots blurred my vision.

How could this slip of a woman have gone through all this over the years? Tears pricked my eyes, but I refrained from letting them out. It wouldn't do us any good if my control broke. I leashed my emotions and blanked all expressions from my face. Unable to stand still, I cursed and jumped to my feet, starting to pace the room.

"How can you live through this? I'm sure there's something you can do. Something *we* can do. Robbie isn't untouchable. We'll call my lawyers, see how we can protect you. I can't believe Robbie has been hurting you for three years." I knitted my fingers behind my neck. "Three years," I barked. "I knew he was a jerk from the way he forced you into that elevator. Fuck. I can't believe I haven't been able to protect you. To stop this madness."

Devon rose to her feet and closed the distance between us. "No. Don't blame yourself. You couldn't have known." My head spun in her direction, but she looked away. She spoke again after a minute. "It only happens a few times a year—"

"Don't. Don't make excuses for him."

Her gaze darted to meet mine. "I'm not. Why do you think I came here yesterday? Because I can't live in fear anymore. I can't live in pain. I want a normal existence. To be able to go out. And to be happy. When I was twenty, I dated this guy from Kentucky. Luke." She sighed and shut her eyes when the memory resurfaced. "When Robbie found out, he jumped him with one of his friends, ordering him to stay away from me. Luke broke up with me the next day, and I never saw him again after that. I'm trapped." Her watery eyes drifted back to mine. "I shouldn't have come here. If Robbie finds out, he'll hurt you. You're in danger, Riley. *I* put you in danger by being reckless."

I ran a hand over my face. "Stop. I'm glad you came to me. I'll let nothing bad happen to you. And he won't hurt me. Don't worry about it." I dropped a kiss on the top of her head, again, the need to touch her strong. A visceral desire to inject doses of strength into her. "We'll get him arrested for assault. You have my word."

"Riley, you're nice and good, but I don't want to put you in the middle of this. I've already risked your safety more than I should. Robbie will do anything to get to me. Anything. You don't want to be on his radar. Believe me."

I pivoted my upper body until I could level our faces.

"Devon, stop. He won't. Let me help you. Let me be here for you."

"No. I refuse to be a burden. You've done enough already. I need to fight Robbie on my own."

I grabbed her hands in mine and offered her a small smile, one I wished would go straight to her heart and make her realize I spoke the truth. How much she could count on me.

Something passed through her glistening eyes. The storms in them lessened. Replaced with something else. Was that hope? Trust? I swallowed hard and squeezed her hands tighter.

"No, you don't have to be alone. Nobody should be."

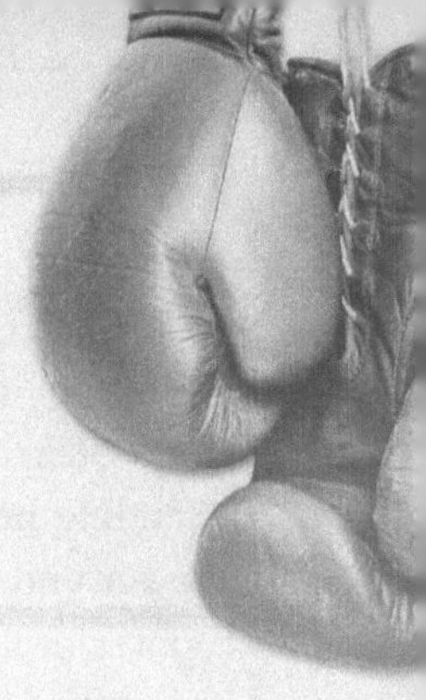

Chapter 15

Devon

Nicole squirmed and bounced on her heels as we entered the bar, just minutes after the show next door had ended. Since she had bumped into him once, a few months back, she had a thing for Sam Stevens. His dark features, serious demeanor, sexy vibe. He was a manly package she had a hard time resisting.

Tonight, the country star was playing a low-key concert. She'd won tickets and brought me along.

"Have you seen the way he smiled at me?" she asked, her arm linked to mine, tugging me toward the bar.

"Nic, he eye-fucked every single girl in that room. It's part of the show. Of his charm."

My friend slapped my arm. "Don't break my fantasy, D. Let me reel into it for a night."

I chuckled and nodded. "Fine."

"Is Anthony working tonight?" she asked, changing the subject and waggling her dark brows.

Hot blood pooled in my cheeks. I used my palms to dissipate the burn.

Anthony and I met a few months back, and we'd been seeing each other in secret a couple of times. He was bartending here, which was the main reason Nicole and I hung around so much. Every time, I pretended to have a sleepover at her house. After what happened when I dated Luke, I had decided to hide my relationships from my brother. I didn't like his over-caring way was starting to tip into overbearing these days. It was suffocating. He argued it was for my safety and that Luke had been a jerk. But we all knew it was bullshit.

Anthony and I weren't dating. Not officially at least. We agreed not to see other people, though. Just the thought of him got my heartbeat to hasten. I had hopes we could be more. Very soon.

"Yes. He is." The blush on my cheeks got warmer. "He should already be——" A strong arm circled my waist, and soft lips traced the length of my nape.

Nicole clapped her hands and squealed. "Going to get us something to drink. You guys enjoy each other while I'm gone."

I pivoted to face my favorite bartender. He looked handsome with his tousled auburn hair and scruffy jaw.

"I was hoping you'd come tonight," he murmured against my lips before kissing me like he really missed me. "Do you think you can spend the night? I've missed you like crazy."

Could my cheeks get any warmer? "I've missed you too." Yes, Anthony was boyfriend material. I locked my hands behind his neck and pulled him closer. "I will. But I have to leave first thing in the morning."

He sighed. "You always do. But hey, I'll take whatever time you give me."

We exchanged grins. His irises sparkled as he kissed the tip of my nose. "I need to get behind the bar, but meet me in an hour, I'll be on a break, and making out with you is at the top of my priority list."

My heart bounced around in my chest.

Nicole brought over some beers, and we took over the dance floor. Every cell in me was giddy at the idea of spending more time with the boy who had the power to capture my heart. Big time.

———

Anthony and I were kissing in the hallway leading to the back door when he jerked his lips from mine and stumbled backward.

I blinked, not sure what had just happened.

A voice I knew too well, spoke from my side. "What do you think you're doing, Devon? I haven't raised you to be a tramp."

I blinked again. "Robbie? What the fuck. What are you doing here?"

Why was my brother here? How did he find me?

He clamped my elbow to lead me away, but Anthony stepped between us, shielding me with his body, his corded forearms tense, ready to throw the first punch.

"She's going nowhere with you, man," he barked. "Let her go or I'll make you."

Okay, Anthony was truly boyfriend material. And he looked super hot defending me.

Robbie bumped his shoulder and clenched his fists. A dark shadow passed in his eyes. Something I had never seen before. It reminded me of Harry...a long time ago.

I shivered.

No, Robbie was nothing like his dad. He cared for me.

He made sure I never missed out on anything. Sure, he was a bit possessive and didn't want me to go out, but as he said, we ought to stick together. We were all the family each of us had left. And that counted for something.

Anthony straightened his demeanor and pushed Robbie back.

My brother showed him his badge and snarled in a threatening voice, "You better walk away from my sister now, or I'll make sure you have no other choice. Did I make myself clear enough?"

Anthony cocked his head to look at me.

No. Robbie had no right to barge in here like this and shatter every good thing in my life.

It was wrong. On so many levels.

I swallowed the lump forming in my throat and shook my head.

Anthony lifted his hands in surrender before him. "No need to go all cop on me, man. We weren't doing anything wrong. Devon and I are—" I waggled a finger to shut him up, begging him with my eyes to say no more.

I pressed a hand to Antony's chest, but my brother yanked it away. Fury built inside me. "Calm down, Robbie." I brought my attention back to Antony. "It's okay. I should probably go anyway."

Moisture welled in my eyes, but I blinked to avoid making a scene. The situation was humiliating enough already.

Anthony stared at me and cupped my cheek with one hand. His voice soothed all my humiliation away, his palm hot against my skin. "Don't go. Stay. I'm not okay with you leaving with him. I could probably call in sick, and we could go to my place. We have plans, remember?"

Robbie's jaw flexed, and his eyes flared with banked anger as he swatted Anthony's hand away from my face.

"Don't you ever touch or even get too close to my sister ever again. I won't warn you twice, dickhead"

"Robbie. Stop," I argued. I spun to face the guy I wished to spend the night with. "I'm…I'm sorry." He looked flabbergasted as Robbie clutched my elbow, tugging me away. *I'll call you*, I mouthed in Anthony's direction over my shoulder.

Once my feet landed on the sidewalk, I jerked my elbow free from my brother's grip. "What the hell, Robbie? You don't get to come in here and tell me what to do. You're not the boss of me. I have a life."

"I thought I said *no boyfriends*," he yelled, rage dripping from every word.

"He's not my boyfriend," I pleaded, hoping it would be enough to tame the anger radiating from his pissed-off self.

"Whatever. His tongue was in your throat. It's enough for me. Jensen was there. Saw the whole thing. He called me to tell me that my sister was acting all slutty in there. I don't want my friends seeing you embarrass yourself—and drag me down with you—like this. And what's that you're wearing? The skirt is too short. What were you thinking, Devon? Or, as usual, you weren't thinking at all, were you? Let's get you home. I'm still on the clock and have more important things to do than prevent you from bringing disgrace to our family. Get a grip on yourself, sis."

I tried to speak but couldn't. The whole reprimand shocked me to silence.

Robbie drove me home in his cruiser and waited while I freshened up.

"Go to sleep. And no more make-out sessions, okay?" Then he grabbed my skirt from the dresser and ripped it apart before discarding it on the floor. "See? I'm doing this for you. One day, you'll thank me."

I nodded. To ease his bad temper. Because I was done fighting tonight. I just wanted this day to be over.

———

The next Friday night, I waited for Anthony to get liquor from the back room. We hadn't seen each other since Robbie forced me away the week before. His eyes lit up when he spotted me. He ran to me, lifting me and spinning me around.

"Fuck, you're beautiful. Are you all right?" he asked, putting me back on my feet. His hands cradled my face as he waited for me to say something.

"Yeah. Forget about my patronizing older brother. He was out of line. I'm sure he had a bad day or something."

"I'm glad you're here. I should ask to leave early so we can spend time together. Your brother is scary as shit. Are you sure he won't come here again tonight?"

I shrugged. "I'll stay by the bar the entire time. I'll watch you work. Forget about him. He can be too much sometimes. He barks but doesn't bite."

Anthony nodded and kissed my lips. "Come on then. Help me bring some bottles to the front."

With my elbows propped on the bar counter, I watched the guy who could easily steal my heart prep drinks. Every time he walked my way, he leaned over the counter to place a kiss on my lips.

If this was what love looked like, I could get used to the idea.

Anthony winked at me, and my insides melted in bursts of glitter."Dev, I've been thinking. I don't want us to be casual anymore." Fireworks erupted inside me. "Would you be—"

A loud cry left my mouth. A strong hand pulled my

hair and dragged me away from the bar, my toes barely touching the floor. What the hell.

My eyes met Anthony's, and in one swift stride, he rounded the bar and came running in my direction.

"Let her go, man," I heard him through the noisy crowd as he hurried after me. "Or I'm calling the cops."

The chilly voice acted like a deadly blizzard around my heart. "I'm the fucking cops." Robbie?

Why was Robbie manhandling me like this? And how did he know I was here? I did my best to be low-key all night.

"Robbie, let go of me. You're hurting me. I'm staying here."

As if he'd been electrocuted, he spun on his heels and slapped me across the face. "Don't you fucking argue with me in front of people."

Stunned, I didn't react.

Alarms blasted inside my head.

Run, they said. But I didn't, trying to make sense of what was happening.

When Anthony reached us, Robbie had already pushed me inside his car, his tires screeching in the dark night as he pulled away from the no-parking space in front of the bar.

My palm rested on my throbbing cheek. My eyes watered. Why did Robbie think hitting me was okay? He saw for years what it did to my mom. Didn't he know better?

"Fucking Jensen called me. Again. Saw you with your boy toy exchanging saliva for hours. He made fun of me, Devon. He said I had no control over my little sister and that I should put a leash on you. I was having a poker game, and the guys roasted me. They nagged me. Said I was too fucking soft. Asked me if I had balls. All because of you and your stupid actions."

He tightened his grip on the steering wheel, his knuckles turning white, and glanced at me with bloodshot eyes.

"Are you drunk?" I asked.

"Not your fucking business. You ruined my night. Now, all I'll hear from the guys is how my sister is a slut. They thought I should give you a lesson. So here I am."

I froze in my seat.

I'd never seen Robbie this upset before.

The whole thing was ridiculous.

We entered my apartment in silence, and Robbie kicked the door shut. His fury seemed to hold the place hostage. Before I could go too far, he shoved me against the wall. Hard. The back of my skull screamed in pain. And I could still feel the stinging sensation of his palm on my cheek.

"You won't act like a brainless child ever again, Devon. I don't have a choice. You won't listen." He ripped my sheer mesh blouse with one hand, almost ruining the black lace tank top underneath, while his other hand held my head so our eyes met. My breathing hitched. There was no humor in his deadly stare. I swallowed, unable to speak my mind. "Why do you think humiliating me is the only way to go? Have you forgotten I have eyes all over town? We're always watching you. Your days of acting like a spoiled, deaf-eared brat are over. From now on, I'm the boss of you."

He let go of me and stepped away.

Anger boiled inside me. I wouldn't let him belittle me. Fuck that.

"You're mad because I'm seeing someone? Someone great? I'm an adult. You don't have a say in my life anymore. You got married, for heaven's sake. Mind your own business."

"I'm a guy. I have needs. It's not the same. And who said I don't get a say in your life? No one. You're *my* responsibility. You're under *my* protection. Shut up. You've made a fool of yourself enough for one night."

"You think I'm an innocent virgin? Wrong. A fragile porcelain doll? Wrong again. I'm not a stupid child. Those days are over. I don't need you or anyone else telling me how to act, Robbie. Go save someone else. I never asked for your protection. I'm good on my own, thank you very much."

Was it something I said, or just the fact that I opposed him? I had no idea. But something snapped in my brother's mind, and the next thing I knew, his hand was around my throat, his body pressing me against the wall.

"Don't you disrespect me. I'm everything to you. I'm the only man you should trust. I'll always make sure you're safe and you have everything you need. I'm doing this because I love you, Devon. You are forcing me to hit you. This is your fault. Don't you know family comes first? And I. Am. Your. Family. Say it," he hollered.

My entire body trembled in terror.

He let go of me, and I landed on my knees on the hardwood floor.

I bit back my tears.

"You're lucky I didn't get my hands on that fucker tonight. Next time you see him, I'll make sure you watch as I break all the bones in his body. One by one. Your call, sis."

Just so that I remembered his words, he raised his steel-tipped boot and kicked me hard in the side. Pain flared like a raging fire, igniting every nerve in my body. My lungs seized halfway, and no air passed through. My abdomen muscles spasmed, and blood stopped flowing to my brain. My vocal cords froze. I couldn't call for help. I was choking on pain.

Robbie offered me a devilish smile. One that froze my blood. He bent down and ruffled my hair. "It will pass, sis. Don't worry." He slithered to the door and let himself out without checking if I was alright.

Only then did my body begin to relax. A scream clawed its way up my throat as hot, scorching tears burned my eyes and carved paths down my cheeks. Darkness swirled around me, thick, suffocating. I searched for something, anything, to anchor me to the present. But it was in vain. I was all alone, with no way to ease the pain.

I rubbed the column of my throat with one hand while clutching my side with the other. My body broke down into heart-wrenching sobs. I tried to muffle them, but they slipped out anyway, breaking through the barrier of my restraint. And shattering the walls I'd built.

I traced the edge of the blanket with my fingertips, searching for that worn spot. The one I'd rubbed so many times between my fingers whenever voices rose in the night back when I was a little girl. The one that still brought me comfort, even after all these years.

I couldn't find it. Panic froze me.

Where was I? Robbie would get to me. He would hurt me. He always did. No matter where I hid.

Stifled screams left the rim of my trembling lips.

My heart jackhammered in my chest.

I cupped my mouth with my hands and rose to a seated position.

High-pitched whimpers broke the silence, rattling each bone in my body.

Images invaded my mind. I blinked them away.

I needed to stay put and not make a sound. To avoid waking the beast.

This was all a dream, I hiccupped. *Just a dream.* Was it, though? Or was I only trying to convince myself?

I perused the room, nothing visible in the darkness.

Why did all of this feel so real? Why was my aching flesh throbbing? And why was air unable to reach my lungs, as if someone had crushed my airways?

Moans escaped my lips as I desperately tried to regain my senses. I needed to find peace again. I needed Riley. I dried my tears as my heart heaved. Rising from the bed, I moved in a trance, my feet guiding me to the only haven I knew—the only one who could keep my demons at bay.

Chapter 16
Riley

A soft knock on my bedroom door woke me up from my deep slumber. I ran a hand over my face and blinked, adjusting my vision to the darkness.

"Riley?"

I lifted myself on my elbows and searched the room, the sound of Devon's voice was powerful enough to chase away the slightest trace of sleep left in me.

"Are you all right?" I asked, my voice rough.

"Yes. No. I-I…I don't know. I'm sorry to bother you. It's…ohmygod…the third time this week. I just… I don't…"

I cleared my throat. "It's fine." I scooted to the side and flipped the covers over. "C'mon. You can sleep in here. I don't mind. Listen, you've been here one week. The trauma won't go away so soon. Give it time. You may need help…professional help. Someone to talk to."

Devon took tentative steps into the bedroom, her ragged breathing the only sound I could hear.

"I...I dreamed of Robbie. The first time he hit me. Then when he broke my bones the first time. It felt...if felt so real. As if I was reliving those moments again. And again. My body hurt. He strangled me. I couldn't breathe. He-he called me names. Dragged me out of that bar. Pulled my hair...it hurt so bad..." She choked on the words as emotions laced through them. "It's silly. I know it's just a stupid nightmare."

She sat on the edge of the mattress next to where I lay.

I grabbed her quivering hand in mine, her touch powerful enough to warm every cell in my body.

"Robbie won't get away with it this time. My lawyers are out for blood. They'll get him arrested. For real. And I'm sure the P.I. we hired we hired will find all the proof needed to convict him too. Trust me. Robbie will never hurt you ever again."

"I-I want to. I really do, but—" Sobs drained her words. I moved back a little, and Devon settled next to me, her back to my front.

"Why are you helping me? You have nothing to gain. How can you be so selfless?"

"The fear that flashed in your eyes on the night we met —when Robbie pushed you into the elevator car—it haunted me for months. I spent days and nights looking for you. Call it a hunch, but I could tell the man was trouble. I won't be at ease until I know he can't hurt you—or anybody else—ever again."

Devon squirmed closer and nestled her body into mine. The scent of her honey shampoo soothed me.

"Can you hold me please?" she asked between sniffles. "I really wanna feel safe right now. I...I need... I need you."

I wound my arms around her waist, and I swallowed hard as she sank herself deeper into my embrace, her hands clutching mine as if she feared I'd vanish.

Entangled together, we both drifted back to sleep.

———

"How are the ribs?" I asked as Devon exited the guest bedroom, dressed in skinny jeans and a teal knitted sweater, one week later.

A smile stretched her lips. "Better. The bruises are fading. Another week and they should be almost invisible." Seriousness took over her face. "About last night—"

She came to my bed in the middle of the night again, nightmares disturbing her peace.

"Hey. It's all good. I'm here whenever you need me."

Devon neared me in the kitchen as I poured two cups of coffee and offered her one. In the two weeks she'd been here, we'd found our way around each other.

We stood face to face.

The air between us warmed. For a few beats, we stared at each other without a word. My eyes traveled from her neck to her lips.

A soft flush crept on her cheeks, and she looked away.

I breathed easier when she stepped outside my bubble, our proximity doing weird things to me.

"Thanks. For the coffee," she said, breathless.

We had yet to talk about this whole living-together situation. It was something we drifted into without asking ourselves questions—at least I didn't. Devon's presence brightened my days, and for some reason, I wasn't in a rush for her to leave.

I loved having her here. In my house. In my life.

She somehow just fit in.

With my back leaning against the counter, I studied her from behind the mug in my hand.

Every time we stood close, my entire body vibrated. The air in the room caught fire. I didn't know if she sensed it too. How many times in the last year did I dream of kissing her? Now that Devon was kinda living with me and we were spending an awful lot of time together, those feelings had returned.

Just like the night we met, the conversation flew easily between us, the smiles we exchanged sincere. I didn't have to try hard around her. It all came to me naturally.

The more of her I saw, the more I craved to know everything about her—what she liked, what she disliked. I wanted to be the one who chased the terror etched in her eyes away for good. To sprinkle happiness into her life. And to make her laugh all the time, the sound highly addictive.

As I stood there, mere feet from her, I had no idea what to do or how to proceed. She'd lived three years in hell. She was jagged, broken.

Would she ever let me near her heart—or her body— or had her jerk of a stepbrother broken her so badly she'd never trust a man again?

"Riley, are you okay?" she asked, watching me with a tipped brow. "You're lost in your thoughts. Far away from here."

I shook my head and snapped back to the present. "Sorry. Just thinking. I'm fine."

"As I was saying, I'll cook dinner tonight. To thank you for all the things you've done for me these past few days. I know it isn't much but—"

I raised a finger to silence her. "You don't have to. If

you want to cook dinner, that's fine, but don't do it because you think you owe me something. I'm choosing to help you, and I'm happy to do it. It's all on me. You asked nothing from me."

I erased the gap between our bodies and touched her elbow.

My heart skipped a beat when Devon's gaze met mine.

We looked at each other in silence for a long time.

The tightness in me returned. How could she be so close and so out of reach at the same time? I cursed at my body for not being able to stay indifferent to everything that was her. Her charm. Her energy. Her beauty. Her strength.

Wishing to regain some of my self-control back, I cleared my throat. "I should go now. I have a meeting. I'll be back at the end of the afternoon. Are you gonna be okay by yourself? Lock all the doors. Double-bolt the main one. It shouldn't take more than a few hours."

I exhaled in relief when Devon nodded, and I left her in the middle of the kitchen, not ready to assess what we could be.

———

An hour later, I met Carter in my office downtown. We had some paperwork to go over together. He walked into the room but halted halfway through, eyeing me.

"You okay?" he asked. "You look like shit? Did you forget to sleep since the last time we met? Or do you have a lady keeping you up all night?" He offered me a crooked smirk.

I huffed and joined my hands on the top of my desk, my shoulders slumping. "I wish."

Carter sprawled in the seat across from me, his pose relaxed, his mind attentive. "What do you mean?"

I scratched my forehead, wondering how to confide in him without breaking the promise I made to Devon about keeping our living situation a secret. Carter frowned, and I told him everything. We had shared so many secrets over the years, I wasn't even worried he'd tell anyone. I really could use a friend right now. And Carter was the only one who knew about her.

"Whoa, I didn't see this one coming," he said, leaning back in his chair when I was done. "Fuck. You were right that night, Ry. We should have searched the place for her. Listened to your gut. Why didn't it occur to us the elevator could reach the basement parking? Damn. I'm sorry I didn't push you to act on your instincts."

I shook my head. "No. Blaming ourselves won't change a thing. But now I can do something about it. No way I'm missing out twice. I checked the guy out. Even the mayor is a fan of him. The entire precinct sees him as untouchable and top-tier."

"She's been living at your place for the last two weeks? How is she doing?"

"Better. I think… Physically at least. Mentally, I don't know. She doesn't open up too much about the beating. Only scarce information here and there. I won't encourage her to confide in me unless she's ready. She's been through too much already. Soon enough, if it all works out, she'll have to testify. I won't add another stressful burden to her life by begging her for horrific details."

"Devon is lucky to have you, man. If you need help with anything, let me know. I know a bit about hell. Those years… Gosh, I wish I could erase them. Clean slate. I'm lucky April came into my life when she did. Probably saved my soul. Or at least, removed the dark cloud hovering over me that made me do stupid shit."

I pondered for a minute. "Savannah would have ruined you, Carter. I'm glad you finally saw her for who she really was before it was too late."

"Yeah." He sighed. "After people I loved left me, and you know my parents, how they are, I just couldn't take it anymore. It seemed like I was drowning, and nothing could keep my head out of the water. But someday, for a reason I can't explain, light came back into my life, and I saw everything as it was. I'm not even sure April knows—well, she's aware of the story—but I'm not certain she understands how bad it really was. And how deep in hell I was buried. Sometimes it feels like I dreamed those years with the devil. As if they're a nightmare I woke up from." He paused and sighed. "Life has a strange way of putting the right people on our road. Remember what I said to you that night. That Devon would come back into your life when you least expect it. Same as April. She appeared at the right time. I'm telling you, man. She saved me and my heart." Carter cleared his throat. "I'm glad I got out of my own hell when I did. I'm sure Devon feels the same. Violence is unforgivable. No matter the form. Does she know you've been obsessed with her for the a long time?"

I rubbed the skin of my nape. "I told her I've been looking for her… But not that she fucking stole my heart that night and I haven't gotten it back yet." I shook my head, wrinkling my nose as the next words left my mouth. "It's still hers, but she has no idea. I never believed in love at first sight… or love most of the time. And yet here I am, obsessed with a stranger I barely know. Go figure. Anyway, I would do about anything for that woman. Anything, man. I swear. Even give that Robbie guy a beating myself."

"Riley Burns getting into a fistfight. I'm not ready to

see that day. Any news from Taylor? He's in the waiting room if you wanna talk to him. He drove me here, said we needed to catch up. He spends all his free time with April when he comes over. They even baked cookies together the other day."

My eyes rounded, then twinkled with mirth.

"I'm telling you. Their friendship is quite something." Carter sighed with a shake of his head. "I'm relegated to third wheel whenever they're together."

"Ha, ha. I love the sound of that. Good for your ego, man. It keeps it in check. Anyway, I'll talk to him later. I hired that P.I. he vouched for. I should hear from him by the end of the week." I fished a stack of papers out of a drawer. "Ready to talk business now? I need to distract myself before I go crazy with murderous thoughts. I'm meeting with Aisha later today. I've worked from home every day for the last two weeks. It's good to be back at the office. Even just for a couple of hours. I have a few things I want to look over with you."

"Let's do this," Carter said, taking the paper I handed him and studying it with a frown.

When I drove back home at the end of the afternoon, I was astounded by the mouthwatering smell of fresh bread and pesto floating through the house. Since the day I moved out after college, years ago, I had never been welcomed into my own home with a home-cooked meal. Sure, I dined at my parents' every now and then, but here, it was the first time. I could easily get used to this.

Devon was focused on her task in the kitchen, soft music playing from a wireless speaker set on the countertop.

Her blonde hair was knotted at the top of her head, a few loose strands grazing her shoulders.

She swayed her hips to the melody of the country ballad, looking joyful.

She had been getting better. A little bit every day. Nighttime was the worst, though. She often woke up screaming or crying, seeking comfort in my arms until the sun rose again outside.

I stood there, like a freaking weirdo, watching her. Relishing her presence. Her optimism. Her bravery. And wanting nothing more than to walk to her, spin her around in my arms, and dance together. The idea of Devon nestled against me flooded me with longing.

I adjusted the crotch of my pants. The last thing this woman needed was for me to have naughty thoughts about her.

I hated myself for even going there in my head.

Reminding myself I could scare her if I didn't let her know I was home, I cleared my throat and devoured the distance between us in four strides, making sure she saw me before getting too close.

"Hey. You're home," she greeted me with a wide smile. "How was your day?"

I loosened the tie around my neck. "Good. It smells amazing in here."

Devon's smile stretched wider. "Careful, it's hot." She pursed her lips and blew on the forkful of pasta she'd just fetched from the simmering pan on the stove—and the vision almost broke me—before bringing the fork to my lips.

I tasted and swallowed the green delicacy and my dirty thoughts in one gulp. "Wow, it's delicious. If you treat me to home-cooked food each time I come home, you'll be on dinner duty every night."

She let out a warm chuckle that filled my heart with heat.

She tasted the food next, and I cupped her face with one hand, careful not to press on her fading bruises. With my thumb, I wiped the sauce off her lips. Devon licked the tip of my finger before bursting into a fit of laughter.

I sucked in a breath. No way she did that. Didn't she know how bad it was for my willpower to have her mouth on any part of my body, fingertips included?

It'd been a while since I'd shared my time with a woman, and right now, Devon was playing a very dangerous game.

My eyes trained on the tilt of her lips—one of the small details that had fascinated me the night we met—for longer than required. I couldn't help myself. I wondered how her mouth would taste if I sampled it—an idea that had been haunting me for the past year. And a year was a fucking long time to yearn for someone.

My body hummed at Devon's sight.

My brain turned into jelly while she stared at me with her gray-blue eyes as if I could do no wrong.

An uncomfortable tension spread inside me, playing with the flimsy restraints I still possessed.

Air shot back to my head, oxygenating my foggy, *unable to think clearly* brain.

Some of my sanity returned with full force as I stepped back from the woman—looking far too beautiful and irresistible for my own good—cooking in my kitchen like she'd been doing it for years. Damn, I had no right to fantasize about her. Not here. Not now. This wasn't what our relationship—no, not a relationship, but a living situation—was about.

With a shake of my head, I flushed my latest dirty thoughts as far down as possible.

The air surrounding us suffocated me. Could Devon feel it too? Could she sense how bad my entire being reacted to her presence? Her closeness? Her charm?

My tongue darted out to moisten my dry lips.

Devon glanced at me with a grin, and it shattered another piece of my control. Was she doing it on purpose, or was it all innocent?

All the sensations I'd felt that night—and had been haunted by for an entire year—came rushing back to me.

My eyes locked onto hers. Just a tilt of my head, and my lips would meet hers. A sense of panic settled deep in my core. Something had changed between us in the last five minutes, but I couldn't pinpoint exactly what it was. Only that the air around us was charged with tiny particles of electricity that hadn't been there before—at least, not since we reconnected.

Walk away, man. Walk away.

For once, the voices in my head didn't sound irrational. They were the words of reason.

Pushing down the lump lodged in my throat, I stepped back, wishing I could rupture the link connecting my heart to my groin.

"Gimme a minute, okay? I'll go change and get us wine." I moved to leave the room but pivoted on my heels at stopped. Before I could analyze my actions, I curled a hand behind Devon's head, and pulled her close, dropping a kiss on the crown of her head. "I'll be right back."

Her scent crushed me. The simple touch of her calmed the storm in my mind but ignited another one in my heart. I was screwed no matter what.

On my way to my bedroom, I fisted my hair with both hands. "What the fuck, man. Don't be an idiot," I said to myself as I changed into a pair of jeans and a simple black T-shirt. "Stop being stupid, stop acting stupid, and stay

our connection hadn't faltered since the night we met and our chemistry was still off the charts, I wouldn't make any assumptions or let myself believe Riley was interested in me that way. A year ago, on that rooftop, he did. I could feel it in every particle of my being back then. But now, even when he looked at me with affection and starving eyes, he always kept me at a safe distance, as if I were fragile. He probably only saw me as this broken woman. The one needing saving after years of abuse and assault by her sibling.

Deep down, if I was honest with myself, I couldn't decide how I hoped our relationship would evolve. We had finally found our rhythm with each other, and it was so precious to me that I would never do anything to jeopardize it.

I studied his expression as he stood before me in the kitchen. Riley looked part-uncomfortable, part-aroused—as if he, too, couldn't decide how to define our relationship—or our co-living status.

Stop, Devon. You're imagining things you wish were true. Was I, though? Was it my imagination—or my deepest wishes—playing tricks on me?

To avoid saying something I might regret later, or doing the things I'd dreamed of for a very long time, I pressed my lips together and stayed silent.

Riley planted a kiss on my forehead, and my body turned into a fireworks show. Maybe my imagination wasn't running so wild after all.

"I'll be right back," he said before turning around and leaving briskly.

After he left the room, I breathed easier, my heart calming its pounding, and my overactive imagination finally taking a break.

Since the night Robbie first laid hands on me, I hadn't

been with any man. After he threatened to kill Anthony, I had refused to poke the bear. The way I broke things off the next morning over the phone, as if he never mattered to me, still tormented me sometimes. Using harsh words, I made sure he'd never contact me again. For his own protection. In the process, I broke both our hearts, and it took mine a while to heal afterward.

I pushed my stepbrother out of my mind, replacing his face with Riley's.

Would I let him kiss me if he ever tried? Would I let him love me if he asked? I was being silly. I wanted to say yes to both, but I feared the idea of a man touching me after all this time would freak me out.

Riley wasn't like any other man I knew, and somehow, I couldn't stop picturing us kissing in my head. When did my mind go from scared to horny? Perhaps the last attack gave me a concussion after all, and a damaged part of my brain was doing all the thinking. Could that be possible, or was I, once again, imagining things that didn't exist?

Anyway, I wasn't here to fall for him or take advantage of his selflessness and huge heart. I was here to heal and find my bearings again. As soon as we heard from the private investigator and lawyers—and Robbie got arrested—I'd go back home...or maybe somewhere else to start fresh. I'd never overstay my welcome for no reason. Nah, I wouldn't live in fear forever. I had to get back to my life at some point.

Could I go back to the life I left behind? I wasn't sure I had what it took to erase the abuse I'd endured behind these walls. I had never truly seen the world. Traveling, redefining myself, and starting fresh excited me. It seemed like a good idea.

California. Texas. Hawaii. I could go anywhere once I was free. I would have no attachments, nothing to keep me from living my life to the fullest. Fall in love. Get a dog. Think about my future. Dream. These were the things I'd never allowed myself to think about before. Soon, if everything unfolded the way Riley said it would, nothing could hold me back anymore. Even though we hadn't known each other for long, a little voice in my head told me I could trust him. That he would truly help me put the past behind me once and for all.

Riley came back, and my eyes swept over him despite myself. Unable to look away, I almost lost my balance. Gosh, he was so handsome. Dressed in a fitted black T-shirt that molded his ripped torso and faded blue jeans hanging low on his hips, I couldn't tear my gaze away. And the guy was barefoot. Stupid me had a weakness for barefoot men who made themselves useful in the kitchen.

Don't think of him that way, I chastised myself. Easier said than done. Even my ovaries ached at the sight of him. It was like they remembered the attraction we shared the night we met and forgot all that had happened since.

While he poured us each a glass of wine, I averted my gaze, trying to regain control of myself. Heat swirled around me, as if someone had cranked up the thermostat.

"I went with red, knowing it could be risky, but I thought we could manage it this time," he said with a wink, reminding me of our meet-cute. "We have a washer on-site if an accident occurs."

h my god, was his voice huskier, or was it just in my head? Nothing made sense anymore. We were on brand-new ground, and I felt completely unprepared to deal with lust this time around.

This thing simmering between us—it was real, my imagination wasn't *that* fertile—messed with my head. And my heart. And other parts of my anatomy I'd forgotten existed until now. A war that pulled me in every direction took place inside me.

I shouldn't be fantasizing about this man. Our living arrangement was temporary, and I was firmly in the friendship zone. Soon, I'd need to move out and learn how to be on my own again. Why was my mind struggling to picture it?

With newfound resolve, I locked away all my attraction for the man generous enough to open his home to a beaten-up stranger like me, and clinked my glass with his.

"Red is our thing." I spoke before I could stop the words from spilling out. Why couldn't I stop myself from flirting with him tonight? Something inside me was defective. That would explain everything, if it were true. At this rate, I'd have to retreat to my room before dinner was even served just to avoid making a fool of myself.

Riley's irises glimmered with something new. I wet my lips with my tongue, and his gaze followed the movement.

The air meant for my brain got caught in my lungs.

The alcohol we drank didn't help me keep my attraction toward my host under wraps. In fact, it seemed to amplify every nerve ending, making me more sensitive to him.

I missed affection. Yes, that could explain my hormones reacting to his closeness, or the warm swirl in my lower belly.

Never breaking eye contact, Riley swallowed and said, "I'm glad you're here, Devon. I really am." Once again, his words—and the way he said my name—scrambled my brain and every inch of my body. Right then, in the middle of his kitchen, I almost melted under the intensity of his stare.

And despite myself, I relished the feeling more than I should—more than I was allowed to.

———

After dinner, we went to the living room, and Riley put on a movie. For some reason, watching TV had become our thing—or maybe just our way of avoiding eye-fucking each other tonight. Watching television was safe. Watching television was what we needed.

"Do you think I could borrow your laptop tomorrow? I have job orders to deal with and probably dozens of work emails to reply to. I would hate losing clients amid everything else."

"I have a second one I don't use in my home office. We'll set it up tomorrow." His eyes found mine. "And if there are more things you need, please tell me. Anything, okay? We could get you a phone. When you're ready."

"Forget it. You've already done more than enough. Thank you for offering…and for the laptop. It means a lot. I'm really grateful for everything you're doing for me."

"It's nothing. I'm just glad I can help. Don't worry about it, okay?"

"It's not nothing. It's everything. I told you once… You're a good man, Riley Burns. And I'm saying it again. I'm thankful to you every second of my life." My voice cracked. Memories of the last beating flashed before my eyes. When Robbie left me for dead, there were a few minutes when I almost wished I had been. Shame burned through me for even thinking it. I hadn't noticed the tears streaming down my face until Riley scooted closer and pulled me against his chest.

He brushed my hair away from my face. "Hey, it's okay. He can't hurt you anymore. I won't let him. You've gotta trust me."

Heart-wrenching sobs—*my* sobs—filled the air. "I know. It's just hard to believe sometimes."

I sank deeper into his embrace, relishing the safety of his arm and the way I just fit against his body, and how it seemed to mold perfectly around mine.

Riley rocked me to peace. The entire time, I clutched his T-shirt in my fists, my only anchor in the cyclone raging inside me.

Before I could understand what I was doing, I rose to my knees and kissed him, the saltiness of my tears mixing with the wine we drank earlier.

I was a quivering mess.

I craved his touch. Right down to my core.

Riley brushed the length of my bottom lip with his thumb for a moment before he claimed my mouth in a slow kiss. Careful at first, but soon with a passion I didn't know existed.

Serenity washed over me, followed by a surge of desire that made my body pulse in ways it hadn't in a long time.

Riley kissed me long and hard, his lips soft and gentle, yet oh so hungry for mine. "I've been dreaming of doing this for over a year," he revealed in a whisper.

I dipped my head, a loud moan escaping my lips.

"Can you feel it too? This thing between us? The pull? It's like the air thickens every time we're in the same room. I wanted to kiss you so badly that night." There. I said it.

His hands found my hips, and I lost myself in the moment, desperate to feel something other than pain. Desperate to feel beautiful again. Desperate to feel precious to someone else.

My palms traveled beneath his shirt, savoring every muscle, ridge, and dip—ready to peel it off—when Riley, his hands still on my hips, leaned back and broke the most earth-shattering kiss of my life.

"Wait. Devon. We shouldn't." He sounded breathless. He writhed to adjust his jeans, and my eyes got transfixed on the bulge beneath his palm. "We can't rush this. You—you need time...to get better."

I blinked, bringing my focus back to him, the back of my eyes raw from the tears I'd cried.

I swallowed hard before breaking the tension hanging between us. "I'm sorry. I...I got lost in my emotions and the moment. Do you want me to go? I can leave. I—"

Riley hauled me onto his lap, our chests just inches apart. "No. Don't leave. I love having you here. Unless you want to... I won't be the guy showing you the door, but I'm not about to take you hostage either." He traced the length of my jaw with his fingers. "God, you're so beautiful. And brave. And your laughter is intoxicating. But your body is still bruised. Rushing this would only make it worse. And I'll never be the man who hurts you, Devon."

I knitted my fingers with his and brought our joined hands to my flaming cheeks.

We stared into each other's souls, letting the beating of our hearts fall in sync.

My voice dropped to a whisper as my brain finally caught up and processed the words he spoke. "You thought about kissing me before?" I asked, feeling bold in front of the man who owned my heart in a million different ways.

"From the moment I laid my eyes on you in that red dress. And every minute since."

A warm flush spread across my cheeks. I used Riley's palms to calm the burn.

"I thought about it a lot too. I'm glad we got it out. You know, I didn't mean to walk away that night. I yearned to be with you. Because you made me smile. And made me believe I deserved better. That I could aspire to a better life...full of love and freedom. I'm sorry it took us a year and those circumstances to find our way back to each other."

"Me too." He kissed my cheek, and I snuggled against him on the couch, enjoying the safety he brought me. "You could never be just a random girl passing through my life, Devon. There's too much at stake…starting with my heart. I can't explain it, but you make me feel things I never thought possible. We need to take it slow, to avoid getting burned."

I traced the shape of his abs with my fingers, savoring the muscles twitching beneath my gentle touch. "I'd like that. You make me feel things I could really get used to. You make me feel alive. It's scary….but enticing too. You're right. Let's not rush what we could be. I'm glad we're on the same wavelength about this. Your presence in my life is precious, and I'll never take it for granted."

———

In the middle of the night, I woke up in the guest bedroom, tucked in my bed, feeling like I rested on a fluffy cloud. I didn't remember falling asleep. We were watching a movie, then I blacked out, sleep overpowering me. Riley must have carried me in here. My lips curled at the thought.

Wrapped in darkness, I could tell it wasn't morning yet. I tossed and turned. In vain. I couldn't doze off anymore. As often happened when I was alone in the dark, a surge of panic crept inside me, dragging those awful memories back to life.

I panted, overwhelmed as motes of panic settled over me.

A knock on the door brought me out of my imminent fit of terror.

"Devon, you awake? Are you all right? You were screaming."

Was I? Ohmygod. With anyone else, I'd be mortified, but for some reason, with Riley, I wasn't ashamed. He had seen me at my lowest point. And cared for me when I thought I'd die.

"Huh…sorry. I didn't realize. Did I wake you?"

"Can I come in?"

I whispered a breathless *Yes*.

Riley moved closer, his hair disheveled, looking hot with sleep still inscribed on his face, he stood next to me, strong enough to quell the panic swirling inside me. "Want me to—?"

"Yes. Please. Hold me."

Without another word, I moved aside, and he glided under the covers, his arms blanketing me from everything, even my nightmares.

Once I felt brave enough, I told him about the idea that had been swirling in my head for the last couple of days. Not that I thought he'd object, but I didn't want to invade his privacy any more than I already had.

My lips grazed his cheeks. "Thank you," I whispered. I sank my body deeper into his embrace.

As if we'd been rehearsing it for years, we fell back to sleep, holding on to each other.

Chapter 18

The rational side of me had gone off gallivanting in space. Every one of my senses was drawn to her. Devon was a magnet—my weakness. The product of my dreams. Before I could overthink any of this, I claimed her mouth, unable to resist her any longer. Her taste was everything I'd ever wished it'd be. And so much more.

"I've been dreaming of doing this for over a year."

Devon dipped her head, her mouth glued to mine, moaning.

"Can you feel it too? This thing between us? The pull? It's like the air thickens every time we're in the same room," she said against my lips. "I wanted to kiss you so badly that night."

Her hands slipped under my shirt, molding to my abs, electrifying my entire being. My breath hitched midway to my lungs. My hands held her hips steady, resisting the temptation to pull her closer, to rub her against the aching part of me.

Reality hit when Devon grabbed the hem of my T-shirt, ready to peel it off me. It was a cold shower to the craving that had sparked between us.

"Wait. Devon. We shouldn't," I said, despising the words as soon as they left my mouth. I adjusted my crotch under her devoted gaze and exhaled, trying to untangle the gelatin ball my rational thoughts had morphed into. "We can't rush this. You—you need time...to get better."

Her face fell. "I'm sorry. I...I got lost in my emotions and the moment. Do you want me to go? I can leave. I—"

Go? No. No, no, no. Why would she think that?

With my hands on her hips, I helped her to my lap. With every breath, her soft chest pressed against mine, messing with my self-control a little more each time.

I looked into her eyes. The deepest part of her soul. "No. Don't leave. I love having you here. Unless you want to... I won't be the guy showing you the door, but I'm not about to take you hostage either." I traced the line of her jaw with my finger, pushing down everything I wanted to tell her but couldn't. It was too soon. She needed time. To heal. And I still couldn't really get the full magnitude of my feelings for her.

With the woman of my dreams nestled in my arms, and after we agreed to take things slow, I pressed play and let the movie roll again. Thirty minutes later, her breathing evened out, and her heartbeat slowed—each thump rever-berating through me.

With my fingers, I combed her hair back, and for a moment, wished my life could always be like this.

I dragged my free hand over my face and I sighed. "For a year, everywhere I went, I looked for you. Always hoping to bump into you. The coffee shop. Work. Every party. Every fundraiser. Every concert. Every time I strolled around town…or went to the park. I could sense you were close, but I had no idea how to reach out to you. I tried. I fucking tried. That night—I watched surveillance footage. I called people. Nobody had seen you leaving. Nobody had seen you leaving. It was like I dreamed you ever existed…that you only existed in my head—and my heart. I'm sorry I didn't find you. I'm sorry you had to go through this…on your own. I spent countless hours in that hotel bar, waiting for you to walk out of the elevator. I was so desperate. Devon, you're the most courageous person I know. Let me be here for you, okay? Not because I feel bad about not being able to rescue you in time, but because I want to. Because you stole my heart that night. And it will never be whole again if…if you're not around."

I shook my head. I'd been a lot of things in my life, but opening my heart raw to someone was probably a first. I had no idea why I felt such a connection with this woman, but her presence alone affected me in ways no one ever had before. It sounded crazy, even to my own ears. I wasn't the type of guy to fall in love easily or get enamored by someone I'd just met. I'd never been in a serious relationship before. I was always too busy, too focused on my career, too caught up in something to really give love the time and nurturing it needed.

This version of me was the opposite of every other version I'd been in the past, and yet, it didn't freak me out as much as it should have. No, it felt right to let her in—to share my house and my life with her. Even if it was just temporary. Would I survive if it was only a short-term arrangement? Right now, as she slept in my arms, I doubted it.

In her sleep, Devon fisted my T-shirt, as if she'd heard

my confessions in her dreams—somehow—and agreed with me.

My pulse raced. I tipped my head back to the ceiling, more confused than I'd been in a very long time.

Once the emotional surge inside me subsided, I lifted her into my arms and carried her to her room. I tucked her in, just like my mom used to when I was a scared little kid afraid of monsters under the bed, then kissed her forehead.

"Don't move out, okay? I'm not ready to lose you again. I just got you back. Let's see where this infatuation between us, this passion, will go. Stay with me. Please."

I stood under the cold water jet, trying to ice my raging hormones and make sense of the way I felt. My body shuddered, longing for release—to get rid of the tension that made me hard as wood yet fragile as crystal. The woman I wanted, the one I craved, slept in the room down the hall. For many reasons, it seemed wrong to jerk myself off. Instead, I went to bed and begged sleep to come and soothe my racing mind.

"No. STOP. Please let go of me."

I rubbed my eyes with my fists. Did someone scream, or was I dreaming? In the darkness of my bedroom, I couldn't tell. *Devon.* Was she having another nightmare? Putting pajama pants on, I hurried to check on her.

After she let me in, I neared her bed, needing to see for myself she really was okay. "Want me to—?"

"Yes. Please. Hold me."

I joined Devon under the covers, hoping my presence alone would keep the monsters in her nightmares at bay. I loved how she could be vulnerable around me. How she didn't have to pretend to be strong all the time when inside, she felt anything but.

Her voice broke the silence just when I was about to fall asleep.

"I've been thinking… I don't wanna be scared forever. There's this lady. I looked her up earlier. She…huh…she teaches a self-defense class to women who've been in abusive relationships. She does at-home lessons." She rolled over, and soon we were lying face to face in the darkness. "If you agree, maybe she could come here a few times. To help me out… I-I don't know. It's just a thought. Take all the time you need to think it over."

I pushed her hair away from her face as if I could gaze into her eyes even if it was too dark to see anything. "I think it's a wonderful idea. I love it. Taylor said he'd be happy to give you pointers whenever you're ready. Just give the woman a call tomorrow and see when she can come over, okay?"

"You won't mind her coming here?"

All I desired at the moment was to kiss her and shut all the hesitant voices in her head. "Never. Devon, I'd do anything to help you heal and move on from your awful past. I love the idea of you getting better at your own pace. Without rushing. And if that lady can come over to help, that's even better. I'm really glad you told me."

Her lips skimmed my cheek, and I had to talk myself out of not kissing her back.

Devon's soft voice shook away all my doubts. Soon I'd be in trouble. Because this woman, with everything she was, had a way to appeal to every part of me. To make me long for her. "Thank you."

Hope dawned on me.

For a future together.

For opening my heart to the possibility of love.

She nestled deeper between my arms, and holding on to her, I fell back asleep, knowing I'd never be able to let her walk away from my life, now that she had imprinted herself into the deepest parts of my heart.

Chapter 19

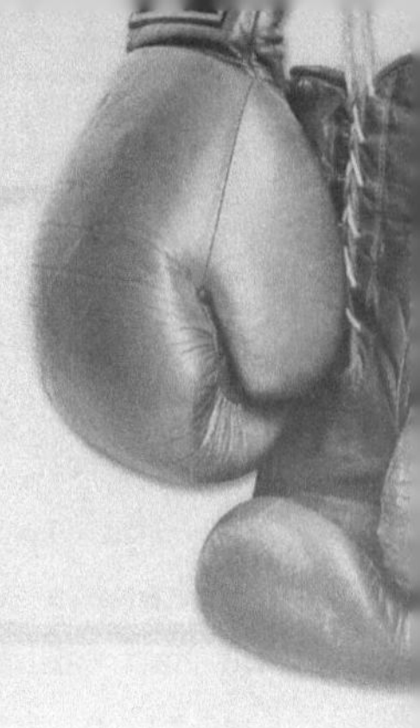

Devon

"**Y**es. Just like that. You gotta aim for the side of the face." Phoebe, the self-defense trainer, moved closer to me and held up my fist. "Always keep your thumb on the outside when you ball your fist, or you'll break it in a fight. And use these knuckles," she said, pointing to the back of my hand. "They're the strong ones. You've gotta hit with them."

I nodded.

Today's session was more about form and learning the basics of self-defense. My body hadn't healed completely, and my ribs were still sore. I couldn't engage in too much of physical activity just yet.

A faint voice resonated in the distance. The sound powerful enough to kill any trace of angst lingering inside me. Today, Riley worked from his home office. He didn't say anything, but I knew he was well aware of how uncomfortable having a stranger over made me. Even if that said stranger came here on my request within three days after I called her. This wonderful man had chosen to stay at home to make sure I would go through my session without freaking out.

When we set up the laptop the other day, he showed me around the back section of the house. An extension he had built to host his home office. Since I arrived, I hadn't explored around, not wanting to invade his privacy any more than I already did. The wide room, as big as my kitchen, living room, and entryway combined counted two windowed walls with a large wooden table in the middle. A mounted TV and a bookshelf filled an entire corner. I raised a brow when I noticed the "relaxation corner," as Riley called it—where a yoga mat lay on the carpeted floor and battery-operated candles flickered on a shelf. Like the rest of his house, the room was clean, spacious, and had a homey feel to it, with a view of the vast backyard that made you feel like you lived outdoors.

"Sometimes, I just crave the calm. The quiet," he had said. "Because in my line of business, noise and late nights are part of the deal." I enjoyed seeing that side of him. Riley was always so organized and efficient. I loved witnessing this more laid-back version of him.

Phoebe continued with her instructions. "Tomorrow, I'll teach you how to use everyday objects you have at home, or even in your purse, as weapons when your strength or the techniques you've learned aren't enough. You'd be surprised the damage you can cause with a ballpoint pen or how you can prevent your aggressor from hurting you with a hardcover book."

The hour-long lesson had already done miracles for my self-confidence as if a door had opened inside me, showing me that I had options. That other women had gone through similar trauma and survived. And thrived now. Phoebe being one such woman.

I was done letting life—or others—decide what was good for me or how and when I needed them to take charge. All my life, since I could remember, I had trusted Robbie with my safety. I'd leaned on him when his dad hit my mother. And again, after our parents passed away.

I was my own star. I had to remember that. And I could shine on my own terms.

The days when I was reliant on other people were over.

If Phoebe taught me anything today, it was that I could do this on my own. I could be the resilient, self-sufficient woman I aspired to be—in every aspect of my life. There was no reason to be scared anymore. No one could ever make me feel inferior or not good enough again. I could hit back. I could fight. And I could win the battle.

Fifteen minutes after she left, Riley joined me as I prepared lunch."How was it?" he asked, picking a celery stick and chewing on it. "You looked happy."

I spun to face him. "I am. Tell me. Did you spy on me, Riley Burns?" I teased.

He shrugged. "I might have. For the sole purpose of making sure you were all right."

His irises sparkled with a mischievous glint.

"I learned many tricks. It remains to be seen if I can apply them in real life."

"You know it's not necessary for you to check that theory, right?"

I offered him a one-shoulder shrug. "I know. But I'll never be unequipped to defend myself ever again. I can't even grasp why I didn't think about going for self-defense classes before." I glanced down, a coil of shame tightening inside me.

Riley cupped my cheek. "You were in survival mode,

Devon. All this time. Don't blame yourself. Never. Brains are not always rational. You took a step back, could think clearly without fearing for your life, and see things from a different perspective. What's important is that you're doing it now. You're changing the narrative. You are taking the matter into your own hands. And that counts for something."

A fog blurred my vision. How could Riley's words always hit me straight in the heart? Where they meant the world to me. Where they made me feel something. Something real.

"Phoebe was great. The hour went by too quickly. It felt good. But more than that, it made me realize I need to be self-reliant. And always count on myself. And strive for my own happiness and safety. I wanna live down my new mantra which is *I'm stronger than my fears.*" A tight ball of emotions bounced around in my stomach. I looked away, unsure how to deal with the emotional surge rising inside me. My bottom lip trembled. I held my breath, trying to ease the turmoil about to wreak havoc in me.

Riley stepped closer, his hands resting on my hips as he leveled his eyes with mine. His Adam's apple bobbed as he watched me. Something resembling fondness waltzed in his gaze. "Dev, you already are all those things. And much more. You have your own business that you've started from scratch. With steady clients. You'd been living on your own for a long time. Providing for yourself. Without anybody's help. Your mother died when you were just a teenager. Yet, you've managed to create this life for yourself. You are successful. And independent. Don't let anyone or anything convince you otherwise. Robbie is the bad seed. The one contaminating your success with his darkness. Not anymore, though. Now you can show the world who you are and excel on your own terms. Without anyone or anything stopping you."

My heart jump-roped in its cage—a little higher each time—with every sentence leaving Riley's mouth.

"You truly believe what you just said?"

"Yep. Every word."

I blinked back tears, using my fingertips to dab the ones escaping."Thank you. This. What…what you said… It means so much. I've never had anyone portray me like this before. Even I have trouble seeing the whole picture. But-but no matter how things turn out, I aspire to a more peaceful life. And a brighter future."

"You're halfway there, Devon. You've already overcome so much. Never forget that."

I watched the man before me for half a minute, wondering how life put him on my road.

My entire self yearned for him. His touch. His kisses. His warmth.

Instead, to calm the desire igniting all my cells, I brought my focus back to the salad I was prepping, all the words Riley delivered taking roots inside me. Filling my heart with pride. And hope.

The next day, Phoebe came over for another lesson.

We had agreed on a three-home visit plan for now. Until my body regained strength and healed completely, and I was ready to leave the house. Then I would attend weekly classes at her women's safety center. And really learn how to defend myself in case I ever encountered violence again.

Never again I'd be a victim.

It was the first step toward the new life I was building for myself.

Riley set the table. "Are you working on that new account after lunch?"

"Yes. I will—" I was mid-sentence when the doorbell rang, and I startled, my words dying away. Vines of tension spread all over my back.

Riley neared me, massaging my shoulders with both hands, and I relished the comfort he brought me. "It's okay. Relax. It's Taylor. He said he would stop by to see you."

"Me?" I asked, my thumb pointing to my chest.

"Yes. You. He wanted to give you some pointers personally, remember? Now that he knows you work with Phoebe, he said he got you something."

I pivoted to stare at him. "What is it?"

Riley shrugged. "No idea. Let's find out." He squeezed my hand. "Wait here. I'll get the door."

In the middle of the kitchen, I stood straight, fidgeting with the bracelet that used to belong to my mother—the only piece of jewelry I never took off.

Men's voices resonated from the entryway. One I recognized. The other I assumed was Taylor's.

"There's no danger," I repeated in a hushed voice. "No one is here to harm you. You. Are. Safe."

My pulse went down a notch.

Some of the knots in my upper back slackened.

Riley walked in with a man tall enough to either be a professional football player or the president's designated bodyguard.

Thanks to the soft smile grazing his lips, he looked more human than sci-fi material.

"Hey," he said in a careful voice. "You must be Devon." His soft voice contrasted with his imposing stature.

I returned his smile. "Yes. Nice to meet you, Taylor."

The man held out his hand, but I pushed it away and hugged him instead.

"Thank you. For everything. I know you're helping me. And I'm thankful. Really."

"I'm just doing my job," Taylor said, offering me a one-shoulder shrug.

I shook my head. "No. Your job is to keep Carter Hills safe. Not chasing after my stepbrother and his potential other victims to help us build a binding case against him."

Taylor leaned back. "Any friends of Riley, I consider them my friends too. And I'm more than happy to help put that jerk behind bars." He paused to fish something out of his jacket pocket. "Here," he said, handing me a keychain. "It's a self-defense tool. When you feel better, I'll show you how to use it. Every woman should own one of those."

I flipped the pen-shaped object between my fingers. "That's really nice of you."

"And if you ever wanna give kickboxing a try, gimme a call. I can teach you." He switched his gaze toward Riley. "You too, Burns. It's never too late to learn how to kick asses."

"We'll see, man," Riley added. "We'll see."

Taylor chuckled.

"Come on," Riley said, "let's go to my office. There's something I wanna run by you."

Taylor nodded. "See you later, Devon."

I'd bet my last dollar Riley wanted the latest news about Robbie but was trying to protect me by keeping me out of the loop.

My heart pounded, its beat roaring in my ears and deafening me at just the thought of my stepbrother, and my lungs overworked as if I'd run ten miles.

I bent forward, my hands propped on my knees, regulating my breathing. With my eyes closed, I ran a hand over my face and exhaled slowly.

Yeah, I still needed to work on the whole *I'm stronger than my fears* thing.

Twenty minutes later, I sat before my borrowed laptop, working on the new project I'd signed up for when Taylor came to say goodbye.

"I hope I'll see you soon," he said.

"Yes," I agreed, motioning to stand. "Thank you again. And I might take you up on your kickboxing lessons offer. I've always wanted to learn how to land a perfect kick. And who knows, I must have some leftover anger simmering inside me from those years of abuse. Channeling it in a constructive way could do me good."

"You got it, girl. Take time to rest and heal, then I'll teach you how to kick asses the proper way."

I hugged Taylor once again, and this time, he rubbed my back gently with his large hand, offering me a bit of comfort.

Riley walked him to the door, and before the bodyguard left, I heard them exchanging words.

"You've got a great one there, Burns. You were right; she's a keeper."

"Let's just say she made a huge impact on me that night."

A little smile tugged at my lips.

Taylor continued. "Whatever you two need, I'm here."

I pictured Riley clapping his shoulder. "Thanks, man. We'll talk soon."

My heart swelled in my chest. I had found a keeper too.

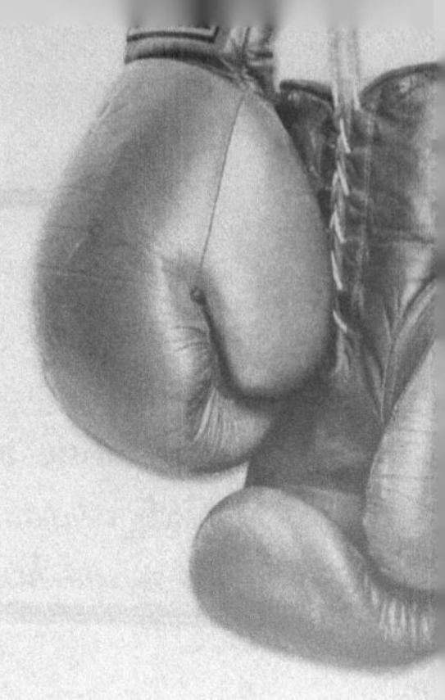

Chapter 20
Riley

"I'm thinking about adopting a dog," I told Devon as we ate breakfast, a few days later.

"Really? What will you do when you're on the road or flying all over the world to join your people on tour?"

I shrugged. "I'll find a way. If I get a dog that isn't too big, maybe I could even bring it along when we travel by bus. I'm sure my mother would love the company from time to time. She often feels lonely in her big house all by herself when she's in town." I put my fork down. "What do you think?"

Devon pointed to her chest with her thumb. "Me? Why does it matter?"

I shrugged again, trying to project a casual demeanor. "Because it does. I want you to choose it with me. I trust your instinct. I've never had a dog before."

"Me neither. You sure?"

"I read somewhere that pets can help people cope with trauma. I've always been alone. Now that you're here, I'm actually enjoying the company. I don't like the idea of being alone anymore. See? It'd be beneficial for both of us." *And because I really want you to get better. And I think a dog could maybe help you. Put a smile on your face. Puppies tend to do that. I'll never get tired of witnessing your happiness. It ruins my heart for any other woman. Because I wanna bask in yours. Every day. For as long as you'll have me.*

Devon squeezed my hand. "You know I'm just here temporarily, right? Until Robbie gets charged for assault."

"Yeah. Sure. But as long as you're here, I'm sure that dog would love the cuddles."

I know I wouldn't object to them either.

We finished breakfast, got dressed, and just when we were about to cross the threshold of the front door, Devon froze.

Her voice vibrated with emotions. "Riley, I…I can't. I-I can't go outside." Her breaths grew quick and shallow, panic flashing in her gray-blue eyes. "No. He-he's out… he's out there… Robbie is out there. Somewhere. He could…ohmygod…he could see me." She shook her head vigorously, her fingernails digging painfully into the skin of my arm.

I turned around to face her and placed my hands on her shoulders, trying to inject doses of serenity into her.

"Then don't. I'll never force you to do something you're not ready for."

Fat tears ran down her porcelain skin. I read all the sorrow passing in her eyes. A lone tear escaped, and every tear she cried always left an indelible mark on my heart.

It'd been almost three weeks since the attack. Most bruises were gone, and Devon had been doing a lot better.

Every day the haunted look in her eyes cleared bit by bit, and she came out of her shell for longer periods of time.

The woman I met last year was returning. Back then, she was dealing with ghosts, but she didn't let them crush her spirits. But this last episode had left her reeling. Now I could see the strength warring with the fear her stepbrother had instilled in her. She would get through this, but it would take time.

With my arm around her, I pulled her to my chest, my lips grazing her forehead. "I found a great place to adopt. Well, June did. Anyway, I'll arrange for the puppies to be brought over. It'll be a fun sight. Geez. No-nonsense June with scampering pups.I'm already laughing just thinking about it."

Devon giggled through her tears. "I can't wait to meet her. She seems like fun. Anyway, you should go by yourself. Don't worry about me. I'm not sure you can get June to bring the litter over."

I tightened my grip around her, unable to let go of her now that her body molded to mine perfectly.

"Why not? When she puts her mind to something, good luck to anyone trying to change it. Let me message June, and we'll see how it goes from there."

Devon lifted her eyes. "Riley, you don't have to do that. Not for me. You've done too much already."

I tucked a curl behind her ear and lifted her chin with my finger until she could stare into my eyes. "I wanna do this. You ask nothing from me. If I get a dog, I want you two to bond. It's important to me. *You're* important to me."

More tears fell down her cheeks, but this time, I couldn't help but notice the soft bend to her lips. It filled my heart with something resembling peace.

———

The next morning, Devon and I sat cross-legged on the living room floor, three mixed-breed puppies running around and chewing on our fingers.

Devon cupped her mouth. "Ohmygod, they are adorable. How will you be able to pick just one?" She lifted a puppy and pressed it to her heart. Her laughter, clear and addictive, resonated throughout the house. All the walls around her had fallen away. Right now, the woman radiated with glee.

I lifted one furry ball up and examined it. "Which one are we supposed to choose? They're all equally cute."

I cringed. I said *we* without thinking. The word just flew out of my mouth in the most natural way. Devon said nothing, and I wondered if she heard me. But then, she added, "Go with your heart." Not, *Let's get this one.*

I studied her as she peppered kisses on the heads of the pups. The black one chewed on the string of her hoodie, and the tri-colored one licked her chin.

Here and now. This was one of those moments I hoped would be etched into my memory forever. The purest expression of love.

The black puppy wriggled free, while the tri-colored one stretched out completely, settling into her arms and soon dozing off. She pressed a gentle kiss behind his ear. I used my phone to snap a picture, wanting to immortalize this simple display of affection forever.

"Okay, I've decided," I whispered as if the normal tone of my voice would wake up the bundle of furry joy. "This one," I said, pointing to the little guy. Or was it a *she?* I scratched my temple. I had no idea.

"Riley—" Devon's eyes turned soft. "You don't have to."

"You two are picture-perfect together. You'll have to

tell me if it's a guy or a girl, though, so we can brainstorm names."

Devon hugged the sleepy animal, murmuring something in its ear. An unfamiliar sensation coiled in my chest and blurred my vision. I blinked hard and moved to my feet, craving a breath of fresh air to unravel all the conflicting emotions swirling inside me.

Chapter 21

Devon

Riley walked in with three mixed-breed dogs in a carrier, and my heart liquified at their sight. I loved animals. They had always brought me comfort. Even if I'd never owned a pet. When I was little, I used to go to the dog park just to scratch the dogs behind their ears or have them give me attention and love.

Right now, it felt like that version of me had come back.

Riley opened the carrier door, and all three puppies came rushing into my lap, licking my face, and sniffing my shirt. A burst of freeing laughter bubbled up.

Riley moved to his feet to chase a puppy trotting around with his shoe. My cheerfulness multiplied when I saw the two playing together. The puppy must have sensed Riley's Chukka boots were worth the money because he refused to give up his treasure. Giggles erupted when I saw the drool smeared on the handcrafted Italian leather shoe.

We both stood tall with tears in our eyes when we sent the two other puppies back, breaking their sibling bond.

"Ohmygod, this is so sad." I hiccupped. "Will they ever forgive us?"

Riley draped an arm around me. "They will. Once they meet their new families."

I bobbed my head. "I hope."

"Hey, what about hope?"

I raised my gaze to his. "What about it?"

"What if we name her Hope? I don't know…" He shrugged. "It kinda fits."

"Don't you want a name that says *guard dog, beware?* Something like Ripper or Roxie?"

He stepped back and eyed me with a scowl. "You think Roxie is a tough female dog name? You're kidding, right?"

He laughed and I followed suit. "A girl in high school was named Roxie. Big and mean and scary. I thought it was fitting."

Riley moved a fist over his mouth, stifling the sound of his laughter. "It's official, Devon. You're the most soft-hearted person I know. Now I can't choose between Roxie and Hope. So, what will it be?" He grew serious again, waiting for me to say something.

I huffed. "Laugh all you want. Even teenage boys were scared of her. I like Hope. As you said, it kinda fits." I brought my attention back to the furball still resting in the crook of my elbow. "What do you think, little pooch? You like Hope?"

She made a cute barking sound, as if to agree.

"It's settled then. Can I leave you two girls alone so I can run some errands and get everything we need for her?"

Hope licked the side of my face.

"Yes. We'll be fine. Won't we, girl? You and I have some cuddling to do."

Riley watched us with something resembling affection and a hint of lust and dropped a kiss on my forehead. "You girls behave," he said with a wink.

I watched him in his red sports car as he pulled out of the driveway, afraid my heart would get too attached to him—big time—if I wasn't careful.

Hope glanced at the door, then at me, from the comfort and safety of my arms.

"I'm screwed, girl. I think it's already too late."

———

In the semi-darkness, we lay on our backs on Riley's bed, Hope sleeping between us. "What did you wanna be growing up when you were a child?" I asked him.

"A singer. Like my father."

"Your father?"

Riley sighed. "Yeah. He's…huh…Curtis Burns."

I blinked, not sure I heard him right. "*The* Curtis Burns?"

He shrugged. "Yep. The one. You're a fan?"

I cringed. "Not really. Sorry…"

He rolled onto his side to watch me. "Don't be." He raked his fingers through his hair. "What did you wanna be when you were just a little girl?"

"A princess. It was my ultimate dream. Thought they were like those invincible women able to change the world with a snap of their fingers. And that they made the world better. And that it mattered."

Riley scooted closer. "In some countries, they are important."

I huffed. "I know. I wanted to be one of those strong and fearless women. And have a horse named Johnny. And a knight kissing me in a tower. Like in fairy tales. It was frivolous. I can see it now."

Riley grabbed my hand. "It's not. Dreams are important. And you've become that princess. Without realizing it. You saved yourself, Dev."

I shook my head. "You kinda did."

"Nah. It was all you." He caressed my cheek with his fingers, his thumb tracing the corner of my lips. "You *are* a princess, Devon. You're one of those strong and courageous women you dreamed of becoming. About that horse… My parents have a stable on their property. None of their horses is named Johnny, but we could go for a ride sometimes. To check the last box on your little Devon's dream list."

I brought a hand over my mouth, not sure what to say. "You would do that for me?"

"I would do anything for you. All you have to do is ask."

His words beelined straight to my heart. "You are that knight, Riley. The one I dreamed of. And you don't even know it because you don't give yourself enough credit."

Ohmygod, could I love him even more than I already did?

Chapter 22
Riley

"My face looks normal. Finally. I never thought I would see this day ever again," Devon said as she climbed onto the bed, wrapped in a red towel a few days later, the curls of her hair loose over her shoulders. In the last month, we'd spent all our free time together since I started working from home as often as possible and only left when I had meetings or events I couldn't miss.

We'd found our pace. Having a woman living with me wasn't as awkward as I'd initially thought, which still surprised me. I had never lived with anyone else before. Ever. Devon had slipped effortlessly into my routine, and I couldn't remember a time when she wasn't part of my life.

After a dozen failed attempts to sleep in the guest bedroom alone, she had moved into my bed full-time, and I had no intention of kicking her out anytime soon.

Every night, we did nothing else but spoon like an old

married couple, bringing each other comfort. Helping each other move out of our own darkness. Devon's pulse beat a frenzied rhythm every time she pressed her back against me, and mine throbbed wildly for the girl who owned it.

Having her in my arms eased some of the attraction I felt for her—at least for now. Deep down, we both hoped for more, but neither of us was brave enough to take the first step that could change the status of our relationship forever.

The air felt charged, the chemistry between us intensifying every time we were together. The more time we spent with each other, the harder it became to pretend that sizzling attraction didn't exist.

Beside me, Devon's grin illuminated her face, and my body ached with a quiet, simmering need. "My ribs are healed too. Being alive has never felt so good."

Her gaze searched mine, and something passed between us. The same electric jolts I felt a year ago. And still felt almost daily.

Devon parted her lips to say something, but the words died on the tip of her tongue.

My own words dissolved in my throat.

I swept my tongue over my lower lip, desperate to bring moisture back to my mouth. She kept her eyes on me the entire time, chewing on her bottom lip as she watched. Our eyes found each other, and all my thoughts deserted me when Devon grinned, the curve of her lips drawing me in.

The bedroom felt brighter, the air lighter around us, yet my chest played a symphony of restrained chaos. For the umpteenth time, I shoved down the desire coiling in every inch of me, each day struggling a little more to keep it locked away.

This woman had a hold on me like no other. She

spoke to my soul, and all control deserted me whenever she came too close. Every cell in my body responded only to her. Her magnetism was irresistible—and I had no desire to resist it. No, nothing about her left me untouched.

She rose to her knees and inched closer, grabbing my hands in hers."Riley, here's the thing… I-I'm not sure I can hold myself back anymore."

Why did my name sound so damn sexy coming from her mouth? I blinked, unsure if I'd heard her right. Devon pursed her lips, her eyes—darker than usual—trained on mine. With an exhaled, she puffed her chest out, arching her body toward me. That was all the permission I needed to stop overthinking everything.

In a single fiery blink, all my self-control dissolved.

With a flick of my wrist, I tugged at the towel around her, unwrapping her like a present, exposing every inch of her fair skin.

My mouth watered. And every inch of me tensed.

"Fuck, you're perfect. I'll be gentle. I promise."

I cradled the back of her head with one hand, tangling my fingers in her hair, while the other rested on the crest of her hipbone. Kneeling before her, I mirrored her stance. My gaze dropped to the pulse point in her neck—the very spot that had entranced me the night we first met. The one I was desperate to devour with my tongue—and with my teeth.

Pulling her to me, I erased every inch of space between our bodies. Her soft skin melted against mine, the heat of her bare flesh washing through me, setting my cells on fire.

Leaning forward, I reveled in the scent of her skin, goose bumps blossoming along my spine, when I traced the length of her neck with my tongue. I groaned my pleasure, the vampiric side of me satisfied. A low whimper left her parted lips, and my body throbbed, ready to burst at the seams.

Devon tasted as good as she looked.

She hummed underneath me as I laid her on her back, my hand fused to one of her perky breasts.

I circled her erect rosy nipples with the pad of my thumb, and she yelped in delight.

Fuck, I could come undone at the sound only.

As slowly as possible, I licked my way down to her collarbone. Her hips bucked off the mattress, and I was a gone man.

Sliding my T-shirt over my head, I sucked in a jagged breath, trying to relax and stretch out the rapture I was free-falling into, wishing it would never end.

Devon's hands pushed my sweatpants down and freed my aching cock. A naughty smile lit her face. "All thick and ready. I like it."

"God, I've waited a year to do this—"

She writhed as I kissed the crook of her neck and the valley between her breasts. Her hand curled around me, the smoothness of her skin contrasting with the steel of mine, playing with the flimsy strings of my composure. With a delicate but firm grip, she worked my erection, and it shattered the very last pieces of my restraint. A guttural growl tore from my throat, our ragged breaths tangling in the air. Fuck, we'd just started, and already I was teetering on the edge.

I shut my eyes for a second, trying to regain some control over my body.

Not ready to surrender myself to her touch just yet, I extended my arm to grab a condom from the nightstand.

Devon snatched the foil packet from my fingers before I could tear it open. "Let me do it. I'm dying to feel you inside me."

My breath hitched, mimicking hers, as I watched her suit up my dick. She eye-fucked it as if it were an *all you can eat* buffet and she was starving. I leaned closer and pushed her hair behind her shoulders before fisting a handful and pulling her toward me. My mouth feasted on hers. My arousal reached new heights. My hard-on twitched, impatient to finally make her mine.

Her soft whimpers and my growls played a symphony I never wanted to end.

With the tip of my length, I teased her soaked center. This was the moment we'd been resisting for weeks. Under my fingertips, shivers rippled along her spine like tiny sparks.

Devon pushed her chest forward, and I sucked on a nipple, enjoying the way she arched her back and tilted her head backward, offering her neck to my greedy mouth.

Carefully, I pushed a finger inside her tight channel, her warmth coating my digit as I glided in and out of her, making the world shrink to just the two of us. She fisted the sheets on both sides of her, and the picture of her, spread naked like this on my bed, broke me.

More than ever, I was certain we were destined to meet that night. No one had ever meant as much to me as she did. No one had ever completed me the way she did.

I plunged forward, needing to take everything she had to offer and to give her everything I was in return.

My scruffy jaw left red abrasions on the porcelain skin of her neck as my tongue continued its exploration.

"Riley, I'll—"

Before she could speak another word, I lowered my hand between her thighs and brushed her swollen clit with my thumb. Her inner walls clamped around my fingers, keeping them prisoners.

I removed my hand just before she went over the edge. It was too soon to abandon ourselves to pleasure just yet.

A loud gasp filled the room.

Every hard inch of me was ready to play.

"Why did you stop? Riley——" Devon said, her voice low and loaded with arousal. "I need this... I...I need you."

I claimed her lips in a bruising kiss while her hands roamed over me, as if she wanted to surrender completely, leaving nothing between us untouched.

"Not yet, baby. I promise to make it up to you. Gosh, you're so perfect."

I dipped my tongue into her mouth, and she met me with hers, each of us trying to gain the upper hand. We moved together like a frenzied tango, breathless and hungry for each other. I leaned back to catch my breath, only for her to nip my bottom lip. The sting of pain mingled with desire, making me ache for her even more.

In one seamless movement, I rolled onto my back, drawing her over me. With both heels planted into the mattress, I pushed myself backward until I rested against the headboard, never releasing my hold on her.

She straddled me and lowered her body slowly, my erection finding its way between her thighs. I groaned as my length disappeared inside her in one thrust.

We both froze.

"Are you all right?" I asked. "Tell me if it's too much, or if you want to stop, or——"

She placed a finger over my lips to silence me. "Stop. I'm fine. Just give me a minute. It's been... gosh, it feels so good... it's been a long time."

I clutched her hips, careful not to leave any bruises. "You sure?"

Devon leaned back, pushing her tits forward, to my

eyes' and hands' greatest delight as I closed my palms around them. "Riley, it really does feel good. It...it feels right." She paused, emotions playing on her features. After a moment, she relaxed against me. "Please don't stop, okay? I think I'll never get enough of that look on your face. You're so handsome. Don't hold back. Rock my world, Riley Burns. Make me see stars." Her words sent a pink flush to her cheeks.

"Gosh, your words alone are enough to drive me wild."

A soft snicker escaped her, but soon her expression morphed, heat and longing shining in her eyes. Her lips trembled. Her body clenched over mine.

"Ride me, baby. I want you to see those stars. And then I want to join you in your galaxy." She moved with deliberate slowness at first, then let her rhythm build, each roll of her hips drawing me closer to a release. "Yeah. Like this. Fuck, you're perfect. Everything okay?"

Devon nodded. "*Yesss.* It's...it's...wow. Give it to me, Riley." She increased the tempo, the sound of skin slapping against skin intoxicating.

I kneaded her round breasts, my hands desperate to touch her everywhere. She cried out my name, I drew in shallow breaths, desperate to hold back, to last longer.

I clenched my jaw, gripping the last threads of self-control I had left.

I had waited so long for this moment. I wasn't ready to let go just yet. Never again would we get to experience our first time together.

My breathing accelerated. I had no more authority over my body. Devon was now in the driver's seat and could do anything she'd like to me. And I fucking loved the idea of her being in charge.

I salivated at the sight of her bouncing tits each time she glided on and off me.

Sweat beaded on her chest. I traced the pearls with the tip of my finger, then lowered my hands until I could clamp the curves of her waist. I held her still while I pounded into her from underneath. Our breaths and our cries blurred together.

Devon straightened herself and clutched the headboard behind me, making it easier for me to lick and bite her hard nipples.

My hands couldn't get enough of her, touching her everywhere, caressing every curve of her body. I trailed my fingers down her back, savoring the goosebumps that blossomed beneath my touch.

I grabbed her ass cheeks, changing the angle, and slid deeper inside her. Her body undulated over mine, tearing me apart and piecing me back together with every motion.

I slipped out of her and moved down on the bed until my face was flush with her pussy. I pushed two fingers inside her and brought her toward her release, while circling her throbbing clit with the tip of my tongue.

Devon whimpered, shaking with pleasure.

With one hand, I stroked myself as I kept playing her with my fingers and tongue.

Her entire body steeled over mine, and her walls tightened around my digits as a first orgasm hit her. She sailed the waves of pleasure rippling through her.

I shut my eyes and stroked my dick faster, chasing my own release, but not quite ready to surrender myself.

Devon moved along my chest, her release leaving a wet trail behind as she turned around and lowered herself over my dick. She rode me again, this time giving me an unobstructed view of her firm ass. Her blonde hair swept her back with each of her movements.

The tingling down my spine was impossible to ignore,

yet I craved more—more of her, more of us, more of everything we were.

"Turn around and lie on your back, I want to watch you come. I want to suck the air out of your lungs when you scream my name. I want to lose myself in your eyes."

Flustered and breathless, Devon did as I said and switched position. I kneeled between her spread legs, admiring the her naked body.

"Every part of you is beautiful."

The flush on her cheeks darkened.

With my fingers intertwined through hers, I brought our joined hands over her head and kissed her with fierceness and hunger until we both had to lean back to catch oxygen. Then I rammed into her, drunk on the sound of her moans each time I filled her to the brim.

She wrapped her legs around my waist, drawing me closer as she met me thrust for thrust. "Riley… I'll… Keep going."

She squeezed my fingers between hers and whispered my name softly. Soon, she tensed and melted into me, coming undone in a way that made her more breathtaking than ever.

I pounded into her twice more, coming with such force I thought my dick would never recover. My body shook, and a loud groan fell from my throat as I surfed the afterquakes of my climax.

Holding the woman who had just undone me in the most beautiful way, I flipped onto my back, bringing her with me. She settled over me, our chests moving in perfect harmony with every shared breath.

"If sex with you is this good, I'm not sure I'll ever be ready for you to move out. I want a do-over every hour of every day." My lips found hers, and our tongues did the talking, neither of us ready to assess the weight of the words I had just unleashed.

Devon's grip on me tightened, and she deepened the kiss, stealing my ability to breathe on my own or to form coherent thoughts.

After my breathing returned to normal, I jumped to my feet and scooped her over my shoulder, her laughter giving my heart wings to fly around in my chest.

"Where are you taking me?" she asked.

I kissed the skin of her ass cheek, just an inch from my face.

"My cave, lady. Where I can have my way with you under the waterfall."

"Oh," she squeaked. "Even your description of a shower is kinda sexy." From her position draped over my shoulder, she pressed a kiss just beneath my shoulder blade. "I can't wait to visit your cave, *caveman*."

"Now I feel like thumping my chest like that jungle guy and swinging from one vine to another, screaming your name so all the other Neanderthals stay far away from what's mine."

I lowered Devon to her feet, and my playfulness dissipated as her bare front slid against mine. Savoring the friction of our skin against each other, a fresh surge of untamed desire and blazing lust coursed through me.

I tipped her chin up with a finger, leveling our eyes. "Devon, I—"

She moved to her tiptoes to kiss me. "Say nothing. Don't ruin this. Just kiss me, okay?"

The space around us thrummed with something heavy with meaning— and hope.

I nodded, unable to tear my eyes away from hers. Even if I tried, I couldn't explain what we were—or what all of this meant.

I drew in a breath and let the real world slip away when our lips met. This time, there was no rush.

I poured all of myself into the kiss, hoping she could feel just how important she was to me, how fortunate I was to have her, and how perfect we were together.

Entangled, we entered the glass shower, never breaking apart. I used the gel June got for her to massage every inch of her exquisite skin, taking my sweet time around her nipples, the curve of her ass, and between her legs.

Kneeling in front of her, I ravished her flesh with my tongue, licking the beads of water running between her round breasts, following their trail down to her navel.

Devon's breathing picked up when I continued my descent toward my ultimate goal. My endgame. My most cherished prize.

A soft yelp then a loud groan tumbled out of her mouth.

With both hands, I placed her against the tiled wall and spread her legs wide. I outlined the length of one thigh with my tongue, taking my sweet time along the bend leading to her sweet spot. Then I did the same treatment to the other leg.

Devon shivered against me.

"Riley… I-I won't… Ohmygod, I can't… I…"

I hadn't even reached my destination yet, and she was already turning into molten lava between my hands.

"Shhh…" I twirled my tongue over her entrance in long strokes. "Let the caveman do his thing, baby."

Some sort of laughter mixed with a sexy grunt tumbled out of her.

"Relax, lady. I promise it'll feel good. Soon. Just enjoy the ride until then."

A new sound rose from her throat, low and trembling, and Devon tilted her head back, spreading her arms on each side of her, as if to keep her balance. I splayed one hand across her belly. She breathed out, and some tension left her.

"Yeah, like this. Let me play your body, baby."

My tongue returned to its mission. My fingers joined the party. A loud cry enveloped us when Devon let go and came against my mouth.

She watched me with stars flashing in her eyes.

"See? I told you," I said, moving toward her on my knees. "I'll always make you see those stars."

The showerhead above us cloaked us in a curtain of steaming water, cutting us off from the rest of the world. I tore open the condom foil I'd brought with me and rolled it over my pulsing length. Devon straddled me, and with her ankles joined behind my back, our chest connecting and our mouths starving, we pleasured each other in a way that blurred the line between passion and tenderness, strangely echoing the intimacy of lovemaking. She wound her arms around my neck as we both moved in sync, lost in our own bubble where no evil could ever harm us.

———

The next morning, we woke up entangled in the sheets, both of us naked and ready for another round. Devon wiggled her ass against my morning wood, toying with my sanity.

My fingers tickled her soft skin under the covers, and I grew harder as she squirmed between my arms.

"Morning," I said, teasing the skin of her neck with my tongue.

Her hand traveled behind her, and she fisted my erection, sending ripples of pleasure through me.

"If you want to play, this playground will be open for

service in five minutes. Don't move, I'll be right back." I kissed her lips, sprang to my feet, and rushed to the bathroom.

I was brushing my teeth when two arms snaked around me from behind, and hungry lips tasted the skin between my shoulder blades.

"I'm tired of waiting," Devon said against my skin, leaving goose bumps behind as her lips trailed downward. "I wanna play. Now."

I spun on the balls of my feet and lifted her so she could loop her legs around my waist.

I pretended to study an invisible watch on my wrist. "Perhaps I could make an exception for you and open the playground early. There are still two minutes to go. But you have a great ass, and your tits taste like heaven." I dropped my head to suck on a nipple just to prove my point. "Yep. Heaven. My favorite taste."

Devon cocked her head back and let out a warm chuckle.

My cells ignited at the contagious sound.

The laughter of this woman had become my ecstasy. The only thing I needed to stay alive.

I joined in as my mouth traveled to her other breast, giving it the same special treatment.

"I want you inside me in the bathtub, on the kitchen table, and against the wall in the living room. From behind. Which one do you pick first?" She twirled a strand of my hair around her finger while she rubbed her naked breasts against my hard chest.

"Under all this gorgeousness, who knew there was a little vixen? This sassy mouth of yours is turning me on. I love women who talk dirty."

"You love my filthy mouth?"

I bobbed my head so fast that I thought it could dislodge from my neck.

"I spent years locked away in my tower, with no chance to truly be myself. I've got a lot of catching up to do."

"In that case… don't hold back, baby. Gimme all you've got."

"First, I want to lick your dick and taste the first drop of your cum on my tongue." She lowered her hand between us and tightened her grip around me.

My breath quickened.

"That's it? Come on… I need more."

"Then I want you to spread me on your kitchen table and feast on me as if I were a buffet sent to you from the gods before fucking me until I forget my name. In all this time, you won't be allowed to come. I'm the one who'll decide when you can let go."

I blinked. Who knew the shy and smart woman I met a year ago was a siren ready to be unleashed? Ready to embrace her newfound freedom?

"Keep going, baby. Don't silence that filthy mouth just yet."

"You asked for it. Next, we'll move to the living room, and you'll enter me from behind, pinching my nipples the entire time you ram into me. I'll see stars again, but you'll hold on because you'll come once we're in the bathtub and I'll suck you dry. How does it sound?"

I was at a loss for words.

So, I said nothing.

Instead, I dived my tongue into her naughty mouth and kissed the hell out of her.

Chapter 23

Devon

"Can we do this every day?" Riley asked from behind me, one hand caressing my stomach from under the water, the other twirling curls of my hair around his finger.

I turned my head until our lips met. "I'd love to. But someday I'll have to go back home. I can't stay here forever. I've already outstayed my welcome."

Riley tensed, his arm anchoring me closer to him, but said nothing.

Sadness rippled through me at the sound of my own words. The emotional tornado taking form inside me surprised me. I loved us together. How we got along. How I felt like I belonged in this man's embrace. How his entire self sated mine with everything I would ever need in this life. How his heart called to mine as his long-lost half who'd just returned.

I blinked back the tears forming in my eyes, my pulse quickening with all the unsaid *what-ifs*.

Riley's lips followed delicate patterns along my nape, scattering soft kisses across every inch of my skin.

It would be so easy to abandon myself to him—utterly and completely.

It would be so easy to let go and become his—now and forever.

He had already turned his life around so much for me. For my safety. And my insecurities.

No way, I'd be able to ask anything else from him.

I had no idea how to define what we were, and I was scared to ask him. Because if he said he preferred us to be a fling after all, it would kill me—and yet, none of his actions screamed we were casual.

I shut my lids and inhaled through my nose.

Could I let myself believe we were *it*? That what we shared was real? Not just an aftermath of him caring for me and saving me from a fate someone else forced on me?

Hope made a barking sound from the little doggy house Riley bought for her.

I'd miss her too when I left. In a short amount of time, Riley and our fur baby had become family to me. *Our.* I shouldn't have let my brain be pleased with those thoughts. Considering them mine would make it ten times harder to leave once Robbie stopped being a threat.

"Puppy time," I said, moving to my feet in the bathtub, freeing myself reluctantly from the man I could see myself going the distance with. "I'll take her outside."

Riley's hand clutched my bare leg, and his eyes snapped toward me. "Devon?"

"Yes?"

"You sure?"

He moved to stand, but I stopped him with a hand on

his shoulder. I sucked in a cleansing breath. "I'll stay in the backyard." I straightened my shoulders. "Far from anyone's inquisitive eyes. I'm sure I can do this. It's about time." Tears rushed to my eyes. I wasn't ready. Still, a quiet longing for space stirred within me, the need to step away from him, even for a moment, pressing against my chest. "I'm stronger than my fears. I gotta do this."

I hadn't stepped a foot outside since I came here all those weeks ago.

I dried off quickly with a towel and, in the bedroom, slipped into the clothes Riley had lent me on the first night. I took a deep whiff of the fabric as tears now rolled freely down my cheeks. As much as I wanted to put distance between us, I also needed to feel him close. I clutched his shirt in an attempt to have a part of him with me. Giving me courage and strength.

In front of the small wooden house with gray shutters and a matching door, its surface marked with paw-shaped holes, I squatted, opening the latch. "Hey, girl. Are you ready to go out?"

Hope made the cutest sound as I pulled her to my heart, and I laughed when she licked my chin, her eyes bright and tail waggling, bottomless joy pouring out from her.

"I've missed you too, baby girl. Come on, let's get you outside, then I'll prepare you a snack."

Ruffling sounds came from the bedroom. Riley was about to join us. With long, hurried strides, I passed his music room. Well, it was more a recreation room with a few guitars on stands along one wall, a pool table in the center with a brown leather couch on the opposite side facing a stoned fireplace. A mounted screen and a bar in the corner completed the look.

The room had dark floors and ceilings and steel-gray

walls, a contrast to the rest of the house. The recreation room fitted more with his bedroom style. Masculine. It screamed testosterone. And long nights of fun. In my hurry, I avoided glancing through the open door. If I did, memories of how he cherished every inch of my body in there yesterday would spring back into my memory, and I really wished to avoid thinking about it for now.

Not relishing the idea of him noticing my distress either, I unbolted the back door without a second thought, stepped outside, and let the fresh air fill my lungs. Sitting on the deck steps, I watched Hope running around. A gentle blend of contentment and peace—and hope—unfurled inside me. Before long, nagging thoughts of leaving this haven of love began to crumble something inside me, and I struggled to hold back my sobs.

Hope came running as if she sensed I needed her affection. I patted her head and tossed the ball she dropped at my feet. She yipped and bounded away, her cheerful self rolling in the grass, not a worry in the world to cloud her day.

When she returned to me, I lifted her in the crook of my arm, her tiny furry body nested against my chest, relishing her warmth and unconditional love. And the strong beating of her heart.

Seconds later, she rested her head on my upper arm and dozed off, her snores calming my agitated self.

"When I go, I'll…I'll miss you, baby girl. You make my days better. You and Riley. I-I'm not sure how I'll manage on my own. I wanted to move far from here to escape Robbie, but now"—I dried the river down my face with the sleeve of my shirt—"I know nothing. I'm getting attached. Too quickly. I'm scared. It…it feels right. What do I do?"

The man my heart beats too strong and too fast for

sat beside me in silence and wrapped me in his arms, the comfort he brought me impossible to translate into words.

His long fingers freed the hair glued to my soaked cheeks.

"Devon. Talk to me. What's wrong? What happened?"

I wiped my nose with the back of my hand, sobs rocking my body. I rested my head against his torso, listening to his heartbeat. Riley said nothing. Without a word, he let me empty the well of my confused emotions. He molded his palm to the back of my head, keeping me close.

With Hope's sleepy body between us, we stayed like that for a very long time.

Until I was tired and barely able to keep my eyes open.

When I thought I'd fall asleep right there, Riley got up and held out his hand for me to grab. I gripped it like a lifeline as he led me to his bedroom. After I lay on my side of the bed, Riley brought one of Hope's blankets and spread it in front of me and positioned the puppy against my heart.

Then he moved to lie down behind me and enveloped me with one arm.

My heart—and my soul—recognized this man as theirs.

And I prayed he felt the same.

Sleep came quickly, the three of us bringing each other love. And much-needed hope.

"Do you wanna talk about it?" Riley asked as we prepped dinner together later that night. "About earlier?"

I shrugged, my focus fully on the vegetables I was

chopping, my hair falling around my face like a curtain, hiding my expressions.

"Don't let thoughts haunt you. I'm here. Whenever you need to vent."

"It's confusing—"

Riley stood beside me, tipping my chin so I could look at him, escaping the shield of my hair.

"Dev, don't let fear creep in between us. We gotta be honest with each other. I want our relationship to rest on a solid foundation."

I blinked. Could he read my deepest thoughts?

I licked my lips, trying to find in me the courage to speak the next words. "You want an *us*?" I asked, my voice unsteady, trying not to get my hopes too high in case he didn't mean what I believed he did.

Riley's hands rested on each side of my neck. "Yeah. An *us*. Isn't it clear enough? I've been longing for an *us* since the first time I saw you." He rubbed a hand over his jaw. "Unless that's not what *you* want. In that case, I…I…" Confusion swirled in his eyes. He frowned, and I hated the idea I put doubts in his mind.

I kissed his lips, silencing him. "I'd love nothing more than *us* being an *us*. Freedom is new to me. And every moment, I'm afraid it will be stolen from me. I fear that this, *us*, is just a mirage. A fragment of my overactive imagination. A dream I'll wake up from. It feels I'm in some sort of coma and living a parallel life because that's the only way my brain can cope with the trauma."

Hope ran our way, chewing on Riley's toe.

He bent over and scooped her up. "Hope and I, we want you in our lives, Devon. This is not a dream. Or an alternate reality. It's real. I crave you so bad in mine that my heart breaks every time I picture you leaving us. Call it what you want, but I believe we belong together. That our *us* is bigger than what our eyes can see. And what our hearts can feel. We were destined to meet that night, I'm sure of it."

I swallowed the slivers of emotions pressing against my airways and splayed my palms across his chest, just over his hammering heart."You mean everything you've just said?"

He nodded, his pupils dark and unblinking, riveted on me.

His Adam's apple bobbed twice, as he had to fight his own emotional overload too.

"Can we take it slow?" I asked. "If we rush into this, I'm scared it will all backfire on us."

He cupped my face with his free hand. "There's no rush, baby. There is nothing I wouldn't do for you, Devon. Nothing. And I didn't mention it earlier, but you went outside on your own this afternoon. It's huge. I don't think you realized how big this is."

Yes, I had done it. I was so caught up in my messy feelings that I didn't celebrate this milestone in my recovery.

Riley was right. I could do this. We could do this. Us. Together.

Fog of tears rose in my eyes, clouding my vision and blurring the image of the man I was falling for, who was standing in front of me, offering me his heart—and everything he was. Without restraint or second thoughts.

I love you, I said in my head.

Riley Burns was all I'd ever yearned for. The only one able to send my heart into a happy frenzy.

His lips reached for mine, promising me everything his words did.

And a whole lot more.

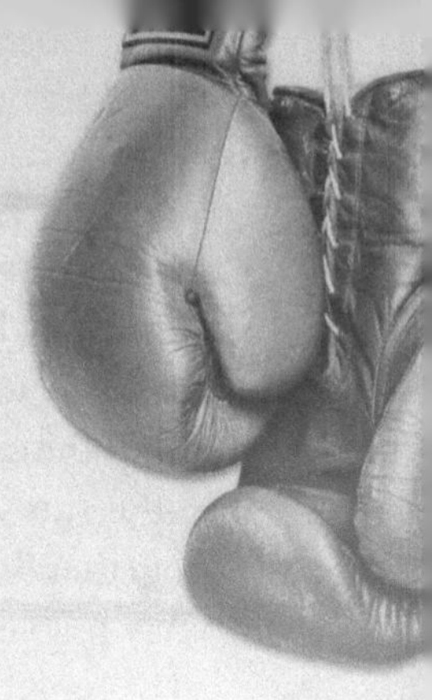

Chapter 24

We were in the kitchen after dinner, barely dressed, eating chocolate mousse that I'd made from scratch when Riley had left home for an hour. I sat on the counter, watching the man I knew I loved fighting me for another spoonful.

"How's work going?" he asked, sparks in his eyes. "Did you sign that new client earlier when I was gone?"

"I did," I said, unable to tame the smile stretching my lips to my ears. "I'm lucky none of my clients canceled their work order after I went MIA for over a week. I've never been so productive before. Must be the idea of never having to look over my shoulder again," I said with a shrug.

Riley nested himself between my legs, and I opened them wider to make room for him. "Your strength. And your talent, Devon. It's all you. You're incredible and hard-working. People feel it when they talk to you. Your charisma is powerful. See? I'm the living proof. One smile my way and I was a goner." His tone turned serious. "I've never been infatuated with any woman before. This relationship thing is new to me too, but as I know with conviction the sun will rise tomorrow, I know we're supposed to be together."

My fingers entangled in his hair.

His breathing accelerated. Yeah, he loved that.

Riley's gaze locked on mine, the air coming in and out of him in quick spurs.

"Devon. There's something I need to say. It's about time I come clean about how I—" His phone went off. He put a finger up. "Just a sec, let me turn it off."

He fished the device out of his pocket. When his eyes landed on the screen, his eyebrows bunched together, his face turning a shade paler."My lawyers," was all he said.

"Ten at night? Must be serious."

He laid a warm kiss on my forehead while all my cells heaved with anticipation. Trepidation anchored itself in my chest, its weight debilitating. I gasped for air, taking hardly any oxygen in. My heart rate thrummed so fast I dreaded it couldn't be contained in my chest cavity much longer. I rubbed the column of my throat, trying to dissipate the tightness.

Riley clutched my thigh, his heat shooting through my bare skin and grounding me.

"Hey, I'm gonna deal with this. Don't worry. I have your back."

I squeezed his hand while he stepped away, praying for good news, but knowing that, no matter what, this call could change my life forever. In so many ways.

"Burns," he answered. Now in business mode, Riley left the kitchen, his phone glued to his ear, and I missed his presence the moment our connection broke, even though a single wall stood between us.

I buried my face in my hands after placing my bowl on the counter beside me.

Breathe, Devon. Just breathe. Trust life. For once, trust it can get better.

Riley's voice made it to my ears from the other room." How…? Yes… I understand." A long pause. Too long for my nerves. "Are you sure?" He gave a soft "Mm-hmm."

My fingernails bit into my palms, pain flaring as they threatened to draw blood.

"What now?" Another excruciating long pause. "We will. Can I do anything tonight?"

Unable to stay in the dark any longer, I jumped from the counter and joined him. His arms opened to blanket me, and his lips lingered on the top of my head as he listened to whatever his lawyer said.

"Please stay in touch. I want to know everything. Don't keep me in the dark… I know you know…" He listened to something his lawyer said and nodded. "Sure… Thank you so much. I appreciate everything. Let me know if I can do something to help." A ghost of a smile curved his lips at something his interlocutor said. "You too. Good night. Thanks again."

He ended the call, breaking our embrace just enough to stare at me.

"Dev, it's over. Robbie is gonna be arrested in an hour. The charges against him are heavy. We have proofs now. Remember the pictures I snapped on the first day you were here? I sent your ripped clothes too. A judge signed a warrant for his arrest earlier today. He'll spend the night in a cell at the precinct. We'll know more tomorrow, but things aren't looking great for him, baby. I trust my guys. If they say it's looking bad for him, then it's looking way worse than bad."

I stood there. Frozen. A hand cupping my mouth. Unable to say a word. My shoulders heaving. My heart thundering. And my body shuddering as if I were cold.

I tried to process the news, but a tug-of-war unfolded in my mind.

Would this be the end for my stepbrother?

Would he really pay for assaulting me this time around?

Would justice prevail? Would I be believed?

So many questions swirled in my head.

"Devon, say something," Riley urged me.

I stuttered, unable to find the right words. "Y—you… huh…sure?"

Of all the things I wanted to ask, this was what I said. God, I needed to get a grip on myself—and my thoughts.

More tears dashed out.

Riley's words finally hit the process center of my brain, and my legs wobbled. This man, the incredible human being I was sharing my life with, caught me before I hit the hardwood floor and carried us to the couch.

He hauled me onto his lap, nuzzling my neck with his arms fastened around me. "Devon, it's good news. Baby, cry all the tears left in your heart because tomorrow is the first day of the rest of your life. You're free."

He smoothed my hair back, and I unshackled the chest of hope I'd kept locked away a long time ago, all my emotions leaping out at the same time. "Wh-where is… he?" I asked once I calmed a little.

"No idea. Why?"

I breathed out. "Because." Could I really do this? "I want to be there when it happens. I gotta witness it when it happens…and…and…see his face. To know it's really real."

Riley straightened from underneath me. "You sure? Baby, you don't have to."

I angled myself to meet his eyes. "I know. But I do. This time, I want proof that it's not just in my head. I want to see it with my own eyes—and talk to him. Show him I'm still standing tall."

Riley sighed. "Although it might not be a good idea, and I'm not sure about you going to him, I too want to look the devil in the eye and dare him to find someone his own size. No one calling himself a man does what he did." He paused and grabbed my hand. "You really sure you wanna do that?"

I nodded. "Yes, I am." I exhaled, pushing all my doubts aside.

Riley studied me for a long second. "Fine, let me see what I can do. Where you go, I'm going. You won't be alone."

I swallowed. "Thanks." I cleared my throat, trying to swallow around the lump that made my voice so strained, while he got up to make the call.

———

On the sidewalk in front of the bar where I used to spend my Friday nights with Nicole, I listened to Taylor as he gave me instructions. Even dressed down in faded jeans and a simple marron T-shirt, the guy looked military grade when he talked business. Massive. And lethal.

"Robbie is in there with two friends. Drew, my P.I., is watching him right now. Pretends to be a patron. Anthony, the owner is—"

My heart tumbled over in my chest. "Anthony? Did you just say Anthony?"

Taylor frowned. "Yes. Why? You know him? Anything we should be aware of?"

I bobbed my head, no words coming out.

"Devon, are you okay?" Riley asked from the other side.

I pushed my uneasiness down. "Yes. No." I shook my head. "Anthony—he might be the same guy I used to kinda date…huh…the one who worked here back wh-when it all started. When Robbie made a scene and dragged me out of the bar. Twice. I-I had to break things off with him, so Robbie wouldn't ruin him. I had no idea he bought the bar. I never saw his again after that…"

A new batch of tears burned the back of my eyes.

"Did he hurt you too?"

I shook my head. "No. God, no. But Robbie said he would hurt Anthony if he caught me with him ever again and make me watch it. I pushed him away to protect him. He cared about me…"

My man harrumphed. "Dev, you don't have to do this." He pulled me against him. "We can go back home now and let the police do their job."

I wiped off my tears with my fingertips. "Nope. I need to be here. I-I'll be okay." I rolled my shoulders back. "See? No more tears. I'm good to go."

Taylor spoke again. "I think Anthony is the same guy. He wanted to kick that bastard out when he walked in, but the P.I. was tailing your brother and convinced Anthony to let it go. Only for tonight." His gaze traveled between Riley and me. "It's good news. It means we have another ally in there. If, huh, anything goes sideways."

Riley stepped forward. "Wait, she's not going in if there's a chance Robbie goes rogue."

Taylor pressed his shoulder with a wide hand. "He won't. We have her back, Burns. We'll do as we said. I'll be in there too. Anyway, it's your call, Devon. You can opt out anytime. The police will be here in less than ten minutes. I can't keep them away any longer. We're already lucky my friend agreed to our little scheme. If you wanna do this, it's now or never."

I blew out a long breath. "I'm ready." I adjusted the hoodie I borrowed because I wanted to bask in Riley's scent while doing what I had planned, and for some unexplainable reason, I felt more at ease and braver wearing his clothes.

"What's my role?" my amazing man asked.

Taylor glanced at him, seriousness glinting in his eyes. "You stay put. And you don't engage with the guy. I'm serious, Burns. I know you wanna kill that motherfucker, because I do too, but if you stir some shit, it won't help our case. So, keep your mouth shut and follow my lead."

Riley closed his eyes and huffed. "I don't like it." He raised his hands before him in surrender. "But hey, I'll do what you asked. Promise."

Taylor nodded. "Gimme a minute to get settled in there, then you and Devon can walk in as two strangers. Devon, you stick to the plan. Let's roll. If the cops get here first, this won't happen."

Riley leaned in to kiss my lips. "Don't do anything stupid. We all have your back. Do what you gotta do. Then we end that fucker."

He squeezed my hand, and a minute after Taylor disappeared into the bar, we followed suit.

Chapter 25

Devon

My heart threatened to run out of my chest. Adrenaline pulsed into my bloodstream at a vertiginous speed. I forgot how to breathe. How to think. All my movements came naturally as if I'd rehearsed them, but I registered none.

My vision adapted to the low light of the room seconds after I walked in. Not much had changed since I was last here.

Riley gave my hand a soft squeeze before letting go, walking beside me but ignoring me at the same time. Still, his presence made me stronger. It soothed some of my angst.

As if I had a sixth sense about him, my eyes found Robbie sitting at a table with two men whom I recognized as his poker buddies. Drunk assholes just like him.

Riley walked away to sit with Taylor and another guy as well-built as him who I assumed to be his P.I. friend.

With careful steps, I approached Robbie's table. One of his friends noticed me before he did. At first, he made a suggestive gesture my way but then seemed to recognize me because he elbowed my stepbrother, busy talking with the third guy.

My blood froze when in slow-motion Robbie turned his head, and his eyes landed on me.

He gave me a slow once-over, glaring at me, bringing his beer bottle to his lips as if he had all the time in the world.

The self-defense lessons I took gave me a sense of power I'd never felt around him before.

In the pocket of my hoodie, I fidgeted with the keychain Taylor gifted me and held it tight between my fingers.

"Well, well, well. Look who the cat has dragged in. Sister dear. *Youuu* got me worried for a moment. I…I knew you wouldn't be able to stay away for long." He shook his head, a satanic laugh passing the rims of his lips. "Guess I should walk *youuu* out of here and put you to bed before you do anything stupid, right?" His gaze darted between his friends. "You know…you know how much I hate it when you interrupt *myyy* night with the guys. It always puts me in a sour mood. I-I'm not tanked enough right now to deal with *youuur* shit. This little disappearance *accct* you put on me quite surprised me to be honest. I-I've been looking all over town for you. Thought you…you ditched me."

Anthony brought another round of beer and placed the bottles on the table, making sure to stay behind Robbie. His eyes found mine for half a second, and he nodded, as if to say this time, he had my back. That he knew the kind of man my stepbrother was.

I swallowed the ball of fire scorching my throat with every breath and drew fragments of courage from deep within me. "Hey, Robbie." My voice sounded steadier than I imagined it would. "I'm here because I need to tell you something." He began to stand, but I lifted a hand between us. "Don't. Your friends can hear what I have to say."

He blinked.

"I just wanted you to see that you didn't break me. No. In fact, every time you've beaten me up, including the last one when you left me for dead, you made me stronger. Tougher. I needed you to see with your own eyes that I'm still here. Standing tall. Not afraid of you. Or what you might do to me. Your woman-beating days are over. You'll never hurt me or anyone else ever again."

Robbie jumped to his feet, clenching his fists at his sides, fury smoldering from his eyes. If a stare could kill, my stepbrother would have annihilated me right here in the middle of the bar.

"*Youuu* shut your stupid mouth, *sisss*. If you say another fucking word, I'll—"

"You'll what, Robbie?" My voice sounded even—and powerful—as I faced the man who made it his mission to destroy me so many times before.

"You think your *smaaart* mouth is cute? I can tell you right now it will…it will get you into trouble. And what the *fuuuck* are you wearing? Whose sweater is this? You-you look stupid." In two strides, he joined me. His fingers wrapped around my wrist, but using the trick I'd learned in self-defense, I used my body weight to knock him down before yanking my arm free from his grip, holding him still on the floor with the sole of my boot for a second before leaping back.

Robbie gawked at me, and blinked, unable to hide his dumbfounded expression.

Had no one stood up to him before?

He schooled his features, and a mask of anger painted his face.

In a quick motion, he rose to his feet and dashed in my direction, his hands aiming for my throat. With a skip to the right, I sidestepped, and he strangled the air instead. And tumbled forward. A few curses left his mouth. His intoxicated brain could probably be to blame for his bad reflexes.

I relished the feel of being fearless in front of Robbie. To witness the loss of his stranglehold on me.

"Wh-what the fuck, *sisss*." He lowered his voice, smoothing his tone. He switched his approach, using a soft voice to bait me. But I knew better. "I…I was worried. I called *youuu*. Went to your place. I thought something happened to you. Called every hospital…"

With my hands in front of me and the keychain secured in my fist, ready to block him if he tried to grab me again, I stared into his eyes, two black abysses sending chills down my spine. I held his gaze. Robbie would never scare me again—and he had to see it for himself. I wouldn't back down. I was done being the target of his anger.

The frantic pounding in my chest gradually eased.

I stretched my neck to relieve some tension, never breaking my stance.

"Don't waste your words, Robbie. You are done hurting people. This is me, here, telling you it's over."

As if on cue, Anthony, Riley, and Taylor came to stand behind me.

"It's time, Devon," my man said, leaning closer.

"What…what are you, *sisss*? A whore?" His eyes took in the three men. "*Ohhh*, I see *youuur* boy toy is still in the picture. Remember the promise I-I made to you the last time I had to extirpate you out of here? Don't say I never warned *youuu*."

Riley tugged at my elbow to pull me back.

Four men dressed in navy clothes with badges hanging around their necks neared the table.

"Robbie Miller?"

My stepbrother brought his flimsy focus toward them. "Not now," he barked. "I-I'm busy. You can wait your turn to buy me a drink." His lips twisted into a creepy smile, amused by an inside joke only he understood. One of the men stepped closer. "Robbie Miller. I'm officer McIntire. And these gentlemen are officers Pearson, Bellhamy, and Cox. You're under arrest."

My stepbrother spun to face them, laughing as if he'd just heard the funniest story. "Yeah, right."

"We have a warrant for your arrest. You can either walk out of here with us calmly, or we can use force," the same man said.

"I'm…I'm a fucking cop," Robbie hollered.

"Oh, we're well aware."

"*Okaaay*, guys. Stop messing with *meee*. Do you know… Do you know who I am? I'm not someone *youuu* wanna mess with. I'm pretty well connected." He laughed it out and snorted. "Anyway, on what basis would you arrest *meee*? For all I know, having a drink after *worrrk* hours with friends isn't a crime."

"Assault and battery."

Robbie's eyes traveled between all of us, and he seemed to sober up."You're fucking kidding me, right? Devon, did you do that? How could you? During all these years, I've been nothing but protective of you. I cared for you. This is how you thank me for watching over your sorry ass for so long?" His attention went back to the officers. "Whatever your heard, whatever she told you, these are lies. All lies," he yelled. "You can't arrest me. Stop with the nonsense. Where are the cameras? Is this a prank?" He stared my way. "Devon, are you in on this? Was this your idea? Say something. Tell them it's a mistake, sis. That I've been nothing but good to you." His laugh grew louder. "You guys looked like the real deal. For a moment I believed it was actually happening."

Officer McIntire started to say something, but I spoke first.

"Robbie, this is no joke. As I told you, you're done hurting me or anyone else."

My stepbrother jumped forward, his hands aiming for my neck again. This time, though, he was held back with a strong grip by two police officers.

"Goodbye, Robbie," I muttered as his eyes turned into deadly weapons.

The policemen exchanged words, but I zoned out.

Riley led me further back as I watched everything unfolding as a spectator, not really registering what was going on. He held me in his arms, close to his heart, as tears of relief rushed out of me. It was done. I had done it. I faced my devil—and came out victorious.

The guys around me talked, but my gaze stayed on Robbie being dragged out of the bar.

"Hey, Devon," Anthony said once Robbie had disappeared through the door, his hands handcuffed behind his back, threatening the officers to sue them. I moved out of Riley's arms and stood in front of my ex-boyfriend. "I'm sorry, Devon. For not standing up to that guy. For letting you go. I...I had no idea. After the last night, he came back with a couple of his guys. Blew off my tires. Threatened me. I was young and stupid. I really cared about you, but they made an impression on me. I lay low after that. I...I know it's no excuse. When you broke things off, even though I liked you, it hurt, but I…" He rubbed the skin of his nape. "I believed you would only bring me trouble and that your brother would never let us be. So, I just forfeited an idea of being with you."

I stood there, my eyes brimming with tears. Every word Anthony spoke reached my heart, shattering and sewing back pieces at the same time.

"I'm sorry, Devon. I hope one day you'll be able to forgive me."

Without thinking, I pulled him into a hug. "I was clueless too. Robbie had never been violent with me before that night. I was young… It excused nothing, but deep down, I never believed he could ever hurt me—" My voice broke, and I drew a few deep breaths in to tame my raging emotions.

With a soothing hand over my upper back, Anthony held me against him. "I'm so relieved you're safe now. Many times, I wanted to reach out, but I was scared of what would happen to you if I did. Your brother, the night he came back to warn me off you, told me he would beat you senseless if I ever contacted you again."

We exchanged healing gazes, a quiet understanding passing between us as our souls accepted the past. We were going to be fine.

"Ready?" Riley asked after we broke apart. I hugged Taylor next before allowing Riley to lead me out of the bar. And back home. To *our* home. To *our* lives. To *our* future.

In the car, the fragile barrier holding my emotions together cracked as my nerves settled. I became an untamable river as tears streamed down my cheeks.

I had done it. I had faced Robbie, and I was the last man—or rather the last woman—standing. I watched him as the officers led him to their cruiser. My eyes took in everything. The handcuffs. The dip in his shoulders when he realized it wasn't some stupid prank. The tightness of his lips when he glared at me one last time. Every single strike that his humiliation and arrest revealed.

A tsunami rose from the bottom of my heart. With my arms folded over my stomach, I leaned forward, the pain unquantifiable. Every cell in me screamed in pain and victory. There was so much I wished I could say, but my words only translated into muffled cries.

My entire body shuddered.

Freedom was a word I never imagined could describe my life. At that epiphany, something inside me detached and dissolved—a weight I'd carried for most of my life. The one that grew when I was still an innocent child with princess dreams. A chain that had coiled around my vital organs to protect them from the pain. And the fear.

Everything shifted in me.

Lightness replaced the darkness. With something brisk. Colorful. Beautiful.

Riley's hand rubbed my back as the tidal waves of grief furloughed inside me.

The man I loved leaned closer, wrapping his arms around me, comforting me with just a touch. "Baby, you did great. I'm proud of you. You are incredible. Let it go now. All of it. And no matter what, I'm here. I'm here for you." His lips lingered on the back of my head.

In the safety of his arms, I did as he said as a mix of happiness, relief, and sadness for the little girl I used to be who could finally put violence behind her—for good— brewed together. Knowing I couldn't get hurt by my stepbrother anymore and that Riley had my back and would never let me dwell in sorrows. And knowing I was stronger than I ever thought possible.

A ghost of a smile curled my lips. The tears flowing out

weren't from pain anymore, but a million other things I was feeling for the very first time.

Tonight, I had done something I had always wished I could do but believed it would never happen. I had been the bigger person. The one who stood up for herself. The one who looked the devil in the eyes and said, *Fuck you, you'll never hurt me ever again.*

I had been that brave princess. The maiden warrior who took charge of her own life and stopped the maleficent force of terror from hurting her any longer.

Never again would I let someone belittle me or make me feel unimportant—or worthless. Nobody would ever again put a hand on me.

A grin slowly emerged as I wiped the tears off my face, the entire night replaying in my mind.

Reality hit me. Hard.

I was finally free.

And this time, it wasn't a dream.

———

When the adrenaline dissipated hours later and sleep came knocking, we went to bed. I had stopped crying a long time ago. For the rest of the night, Riley and I cuddled on the couch, his fingers playing with the curls of my hair, like he did every time we were relaxing together.

Something Riley said earlier flashed in my mind as I got comfortable under the covers. "Remember seconds before your lawyers called, you started telling me something. About coming clean... I wish I knew what it was about, you never finished that thought."

He scooted closer and hauled me on top of him, our face a hair's breadth apart, my breasts pressing against his hard chest, loving how our bodies molded together. "You sure you're ready to hear me out?" he asked, his voice soft as dripping honey, sending tingles along each of my vertebrae, the tips of his fingers awakening goose bumps all over my back. "The night has already been quite emotional…"

His eyes brightened in the darkness, the only light coming from the silver moonbeam shining through the giant window in the hallway. His stare enveloped me in a cocoon I never wanted to leave.

"I'm not that tired anymore. We should celebrate. I think I could maybe—" I lowered myself, kissing my way down his body. Riley's breath hitched, and he tensed when my tongue followed the path to his manhood, ready to kick in the celebrations. I had everything to be thankful for. And I owed all this gratefulness to this man. *My* handsome man.

His dick twitched when my palm curled around it, working him as my tongue circled the tip.

With a jagged breath, Riley fisted my hair as I continued my discovery of his anatomy, taking all of him inside my mouth.

I pumped him faster while my tongue lapped at him.

"Fuck, Dev. That's not how I wanted to tell you."

I raised my eyes to meet his, savoring him without pause. "Tell me what?"

He sprang to a seated position, forcing me to let go of him.

I kneeled in front of him, noticing sternness in his expression.

"Everything all right? Are you okay?" I paused. My heart dipped in my chest, and I swallowed before speaking again. With everything that went down tonight, I never took the time to make sure he was all right. That he was okay with me facing Robbie the way I did. And Anthony. And the cops. And my stepbrother insulting me and calling me names. "Are we…are we okay?"

Riley mirrored my stance and breezed closer, never breaking eye contact.

Millions of knots coiled around my stomach, so tight the pain spread to my skull.

I pushed back, scared of the words about to leave his mouth. Before I could move too far, Riley intertwined his fingers through mine.

"Devon, I didn't mean to tell you this when you had my dick in your mouth or after you went through an avalanche of emotions earlier, but I can't hold it anymore. I'm too fucking far gone."

I sucked in a breath.

"Wh-what do you mean?"

"We said we'd be honest with each other. So, hear me out, okay?"

"O-okay," I whispered, not sure where this conversation was heading.

Riley's gaze searched mine.

My heart skipped a beat, its rhythm offbeat.

I chewed on my lips while I waited for whatever word that would come out of his mouth.

But then something passed between us, and tingles of lust filled his eyes.

His lips bent at the corners.

The air around us felt warmer. Cozier.

My pulse slowed down, finding its tempo.

My chest expanded as if a beautiful flower bloomed and filled the space.

Every part of me shifted in place.

"Devon, I love you. God, I do. The set-up isn't romantic, and the moment is random, but I can't have sex with you without being honest first. I love *you*. All of you. You are all I think about. It may sound too soon, or rushed, but it's not. Our story is a year long… Even if we didn't see each other for most of it, you were on my mind the entire time. I dreamed of you every night. I wished for you every minute of every waking hour. When you came here asking for my help, I thanked all the saints above for bringing you back to me because no one will ever care for you the way I want to. Because no one will ever love you the way I do… the way I'm meant to. I've never been into romance or into forever and always, but now I know why. I was waiting for *you*. The whole time, I couldn't believe in love because you existed, and it had to be you…it had to be with you. My heart knew it all along. It just kept it to itself."

Tears blurred my vision, etching hot trenches into my skin.

"Riley—" I tried to voice my feelings, but heavy sobs made it impossible to express myself.

This time, I wasn't crying from pain or relief, but from elation.

Riley framed my face with his hands, the pads of his thumbs clearing my sight.

"I love you, Devon. And this will never change."

He kissed my eyelids, the tip of my nose, my cheek-bones, my jaws, swallowing every drop that leaked from my eyes, before fusing his mouth to mine.

The entire fortress I'd erected all around myself—and my heart—shattered to pieces.

I didn't require protection anymore.

I had love, and with this feeling alone, I could conquer the world.

"I love you," I whispered with a croaky voice, my vocal cords raw with all the tears I'd cried tonight. "I knew I loved you when you offered to wash my hair. And when you picked Hope because she and I had the best connection that day. You showed me over and over how selfless, caring, honest, good, and gentle you are. I'll never take any of this for granted because it's truly something special. You are special, Riley Burns. You make the world around you a better place. I'm the happiest woman on Earth that you chose to shine your light on me. That you chose me to love." I wiped a fresh batch of hot tears. "I love you so much. You're amazing. I'm gonna love the shit out of you right now. Thank you for believing in me. And caring. And coming tonight. I never wanna feel different from the way I feel right now. With you."

Riley's palm rested on the back of my head as he stared into my eyes. Into my heart. Into my soul.

His lips parted, but he said nothing. Instead, he dived forward and ravaged my mouth with his, injecting me with dozens of love promises as his tongue waltzed with mine. I lay back, pulling my starving man down with me in one smooth motion.

He kneaded one of my breasts with his other hand, rolling my stiff nipple between his thumb and index finger. I purred against his lips, desire shooting in all directions inside me. Heat pooled in my lower belly and wetness between my legs. My toes curled. My entire body now only responded to the touch of the man it recognized as the keeper of its heart.

I tilted my head back, relishing the way Riley's teeth nipped the skin from my chin down to my collarbone and up again.

I dug my fingernails in his ass cheeks, pulling him flush to me, his erection pressing against my lower belly.

It was as if our hands discovered each other for the very first time. As if it knew this was forever, and we needed to familiarize ourselves with every curve, every scar, every ridge.

"Fuck, Devon. You taste even better. How is it even possible?" He bowed his head lower, sucking on one nipple, then the other. I couldn't contain the ecstasy bursting inside me.

"Riley. I need you. Now." He pushed a finger inside me, his eyes never leaving mine. "Oh yes. Oh… It feels so good. Don't stop—" I sucked in a long breath, trying to stay anchored to the present. And to this earth. "I love you. I love you so much," I moaned while his thumb busied itself circling my pulsing bundle of nerves, bringing me to heaven and back.

With an extended arm, I reached for the nightstand to grab a condom, and with hands shaking from expectation and so much lust, I suited his pulsing hard-on, just in time before he slid home—where he belonged. I shivered at the sensation of us connecting in the rawest way possible, promising each other more than any word could. I never knew love could feel this good, this freeing, and this life-shattering.

Riley laid me on my back and laced his fingers through mine, bringing our joined hands on each side of my head as he glided in and out of me at an addictive pace, watching me watch him.

"I love you," he whispered, a secret only we shared. "I love you so very much."

I locked my ankles around his back, meeting him thrust for thrust.

Riley kissed the valley between my breasts. He kissed my jaw, my lids, my shoulder.

Basking in his love, I felt more powerful and beautiful than I ever did before.

I freed my hands from his and propped myself up on one elbow, looping my other arm around his neck, craving the contact of his lips on mine.

Riley supported my back, deepening the kiss until I felt

it down to my toes. "Devon, I won't last long. Come. Come with me, baby."

I returned to my back while he pushed himself to his knees, gripping my hipbone, my knees falling on either side. Riley pounded harder. Faster. Whimpers left my mouth. I closed my eyes, every sensation inside me magnifying, my head light, my body experiencing a nirvana it never had before.

Riley pulled back, and bracing my legs over his shoulders, he moved down on me as his greedy tongue laved my center in keen strokes.

A shiver formed at the tip of my spine.

"I'm almost there," I cried.

He moved between my legs, pushing his burning flesh inside me in one final push as we both climaxed together, swimming in bliss. Love bliss.

He emptied himself in strong jolts, a guttural growl breaking the silence surrounding us.

"Devon. I'm in love with you. This is real. And we're real." After he kissed every inch of my damp skin again, he rose to his feet, bringing me with him. We let the warm water of the shower rinse us while we kissed as if it were the first time.

Exhausted, but with a hopeful heart, we buried ourselves under the covers, Riley's heartbeat the only melody I needed for the rest of my life. The only sound able to bring me peace. A love song promising us a blissful future.

My pulse finally decreased as sleep chased me in the arms of the man who loved me with everything he was. And everything he had.

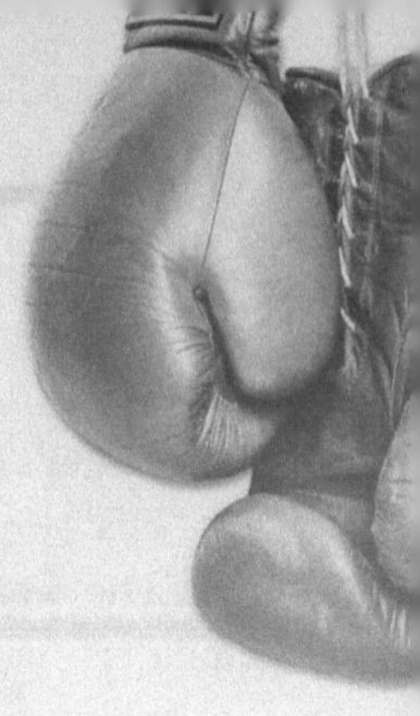

Chapter 26
Riley

"Are you sure your mother wants me to come with you to this dinner? And what are we gonna tell your parents? That we're dating after I moved in with you over a month ago, the same night my step-brother beat the shit out of me, and that since then, I haven't stepped a foot outside except to confront him the night he got arrested, scared a cruiser would drive past your house and they'd recognize me?" I arched a brow. "They'll stage an intervention. Think you went crazy and try to force some sense into you."

Devon looked adorable with all her unjustified doubts.

How could she not see I was so into her? And that I was in for the long run. That nothing she or anyone else could say would prevent me from caring for her and being there for her. And loving her with every piece of my heart.

My parents' opinion didn't matter. It wasn't as if my

father had valuable tips to share in the relationship depart-ment anyway.

She pouted, and I let out a soft laugh, kissing her lips so she wouldn't believe I was making fun of her.

"First, we don't owe anyone an explanation. You're my girl. The woman I love." I pushed her hair behind her shoulders with fingers itching to touch her soft skin. Everything about this woman mesmerized me. Most of the time, I still couldn't believe she was here with me. "The details are ours, and don't have to be shared. Second, my lawyers told us earlier the charges against Robbie are multiplying. They convinced the woman he assaulted in Memphis to press charges too. In addition to that dancer and the two women who came forward already. There are five of you now. They are still tracking down the ex-wife to see if he assaulted her too. None of Robbie's little Nashville police friends can help him out this time. You weren't his only side-hustle, baby. There might be more. Third, as long as you're by my side, nothing will happen to you. Gus, one of Taylor's guys, will shadow you any time you have to go out. You can't lock yourself in forever. Soon, you'll start living again. When you're ready. There's so much out there I wanna show you, and I can't wait for you to meet my friends. And my music family. Carter, April, Aisha, June, Sam, Dahlia, Stud. All of them. They're not just business partners; they mean the world to me. They are my people. Don't give Robbie that much power over you."

Devon's eyes clouded, and she blinked. "I won't. Told you. I'm stronger than my fears. I wanna embrace life as it's meant to be. I'm getting there." She offered me a shy smile. "Riley, how did I end up with a man like you? I'm not sure what I did to deserve your love and affection. And strength. And selfless heart. I've been imposing myself on your life, and you never asked me to move out or anything. You never asked for anything in return."

I failed to contain my grin as it took over my face.

"Because I want you here. Maybe I'm crazy, but deep down, it feels like I've known you all my life. As if I've been waiting for you. You'll think I'm silly—"

Devon kissed my lips briefly to shut me up. "It's not silly. The moment my eyes landed on you in that bar, something unfolded inside me. As if I'd found the missing piece of my heart that I'd been waiting forever to retrieve. The one that had withered away after my mother passed. The most important part holding the secret to my happiness."

I leaned in to kiss the bare curve of her shoulder.

"I love you, Devon. Stop worrying about what my parents will think then. I feel the same. If you don't wanna go, I won't either. My father and I aren't on speaking terms these days."

"What happened?"

"I've already told you my father is Curtis Burns, the country legend." She nodded. "Growing up, he was my hero. He'd take me everywhere with him. On the road, at award shows. From the day I was born, country music has run through my veins. All I've ever wanted was to follow in his footsteps. But I can't sing for shit, so I decided that I'd be better off as a manager. It suits me better anyway. I'm a people person. Two weeks before you appeared on my doorstep, I'd learned that my father had approached one singer I'd had my sights on for a very long time and signed him to his new management firm, disregarding me. My father is a country singer, not an agent. And the night you came back into my life, I was drowning my sorrows after I'd learned that Anderson Ford—the singer I thought would sign with me—is in fact my father's lovechild. I...I didn't know. My parents had been keeping him a secret from me all this time. For my entire life, I had a brother and never knew he existed."

"Wait. Your mother knew?"

I nodded. "My father told her when he found out. They separated when I was about four or five years old, I think. I have no memory of that time. My dad was gone on tour a lot. Sometimes we followed him around, but my mother wanted to give me a normal life, so we stayed home more often than not, and she enrolled me in school with all the regular childhood stuff. My father had an affair during that time, but later that year, my parents got back together, renewed their wedding vows, and have never left each other's side since."

"What was the point of telling you now?"

"Dear Dad was afraid I'd learn the truth, and I'd mess with his youngest son's career out of anger. Or hurt."

"That's ridiculous. There's no darkness in you. Evil isn't in your blood. Believe me, I know what it looks like." A memory passed in Devon's gaze, but this time, she chased it away with a blink of her eye, her smile returning, and her gaze emptied of the terror that had lingered in them for so long. Even the night we met, there were hints of it. I just hadn't known at the time what it meant. "What now?"

I shrugged. "Nothing. I'm not ready to face my father yet. It was a low blow when he poached Anderson from me. I was supposed to sign him a while back, but then he found out who his father was and freaked out. He didn't return my calls for the longest time, not wanting to be caught between Curtis and me after Curtis appeared in his life and admitted the truth. My own father played me. Now I feel stupid for not knowing we were half-siblings. We look a lot alike, Anderson and I. See? Epic shitshow."

Devon nested herself between my arms. "Fine, you've convinced me. I'll hold your hand the entire time if it helps you. I'll be by your side, no matter what. It's my turn to be there for you. If you wanna leave, just say the word, and we'll go. No questions asked. You won't have to face him by yourself. You have me now. And I'll always have your back."

"Thanks. I enjoy having you around—and in my bed."

I kissed her lips, and Devon circled my neck with her arms, deepening the kiss. My entire body pulsed against hers. Electrifying, shooting fireworks, igniting from the marrow of my bones. We made out a little longer. I traced the seam between her legs with my thumb, and she shuddered.

"Not now," she said. "Or we'll be late. Tonight, I'll be your naked subject, so you'll be able to pleasure me in any way you like."

"Fuck, Dev," I growled, removing my hand.

Shegasped and writhed against me at the withdrawal of my sinful fingers. "Riley—"

"Tonight, baby. Your words."

We broke apart, panting, pressing our foreheads together, both of us radiating enough sexual energy to put my house on fire. When our heavy breathing slowed to normal, I spoke again. "Now turn around, I'll zip you up."

Today, Devon wore a simple black dress that hugged all her curves. It contrasted with her blonde locks and made it impossible for me to look elsewhere.

She twirled around, and it reminded me of the night we met. The glint in her eye had returned. It took almost a month, but now it was there full-time. It lit up even brighter when her gaze landed on me, which made every one of my cells long for her.

"You look fabulous. Are you ready?"

"Yeah, let's do this. Let's face our fears together." We laced our fingers and halted on the front porch. Devon's grip tightened. She inhaled. And exhaled. Inhaled. And exhaled. The entire time, my eyes stayed fixed on her, watching her be brave.

"You okay?" I asked, bringing our joined hands to my lips and kissing her knuckles.

She breathed out a whispered "Yes." She swallowed, firmed her back, and stepped forward with a firm resolve. On her tiptoes, she kissed my cheek and patted Hope's head with her free hand. "You guys are all I'll ever need. Let's do this," she said, echoing my own words.

Hand in hand, we left the house—Devon's second time since the night she came here all banged up—and my heart felt much lighter as my woman walked beside me. This time, she was the one injecting me doses of strength by being by my side, and making me face my own demons.

"You did it," I whispered in her ear as I closed the passenger door once she settled in the car. "I'm so proud of you, baby."

"I love you, Riley. With every fiber of my heart. Thank you. For believing in me. And loving me with no conditions."

I kissed her one last time before placing Hope in the carrier I kept behind my seat.

———

I inhaled through my mouth as I knocked on the front door of my parents' mansion. Money could buy lots of things, but I preferred a low-key life over the extravaganza I was born into.

The only expense I splurged on, in the last year, was my car.

Lodged in a dead-end street, my parents had football players and other country music stars as neighbors. My childhood home looked the same as it always had. A cobblestone path leading to the front door. White columns on each side. Bushes trimmed to perfection and a stable on the left.

My mother, dressed in a dark purple suit, a pearl necklace around her neck, with her strawberry-blonde hair tied in a low ponytail, opened the door. Her eyes darted to Devon before they even reached me.

She cupped her heart as she looked at my girlfriend, standing there, her hand firmly anchored to mine. "Oh, Riley darling, she's beautiful. I'm glad to finally meet the woman sharing your life. What's your name, dear?"

Devon's eyes rounded. I squeezed her hand, hoping she'd understand I had nothing to do with my mother's meddling.

That stupid sixth sense again.

Oh, yes. And that microchip.

My throat closed. Then it relaxed.

My eyes met my woman's. We shared a glance filled with amusement. And love—true love.

"Mama, this is Devon. Devon, this is my mother, Robin."

"It's nice to meet you, Mrs. Burns. Riley told me so much about you."

"Call me Robin." My mother tugged at her hand and pulled her into the house. "I hope Riley is nice to you. Call it a mother's intuition, but I can already tell you bring him joy. That smile you see on his face, it looks genuine now. And I've been waiting a long time to see this boy of mine happy. And in love."

I rolled my eyes. *Please, Mama, stop embarrassing me.*

"Your son has been nothing but amazing to me, Robin.

You raised him well. You should be proud. He's a good man. The best I know."

Our gazes collided. Devon sucked all the air from my lungs as she stared at me with so much heat in her eyes. And lust. And love. I averted mine, breaking the spell, hot waves washing over me. I needed a drink. Stat.

As my mother entertained Devon with another one of my childhood stories, embarrassing ones at that, I placed Hope by their feet in the little bed we brought over and escaped to the library. The room was huge with floor-to-ceiling windows, a wall filled to the brim with hardback classic novels, biographies, and other nonfiction works, an emerald-green set of velvet sofas, a stone-framed fireplace, and a bar.

I made a beeline for the bar, desperate to tame the prickle in my throat with something stronger.

I sensed him before I could see him. My father. "Hello, son." His Southern drawl was strong. The one from Oklahoma he never lost and that people all around the globe found charming every time he sat for interviews.

"Hey." I nodded, trying to act cool and distant.

"I'm glad you came. We have much to talk about, you and I. It's about time."

I shook my head as I filled my tumbler higher than good manners allowed.

"I'm not sure I'm ready to have that conversation just yet. Right now, I can't decide if I'm more upset at my dad who got a woman other than my mother pregnant when I was a child or at the country music star who signed a contract with an artist I had my sight for a fucking long time on behind my back, too scared to come clean about what he did over twenty years ago."

"I know you're upset. I understand, but I hope, one day, you'll find it in you to forgive me," my father said, his shoulders slouching forward and sadness brimming in his eyes, the same color as mine, looking ten years older than usual.

I cleared my throat, pushing the smithereens of betrayal down. "I will. I just need some time to process everything. When I'm ready, we'll talk. Perhaps Anderson and I could even have some sort of relationship one day. Not now, though. It's too soon." A sarcastic laugh bubbled out. "To think all my life I've wished for a brother. You knew it. And you kept him from me. Even though I have no idea how I would've reacted. This is fucked up. I can't decide if it's a good thing or a joke that life—and maybe you—are playing on me."

After I spoke the last words, I let out a harsh breath, and some of the tension in my back dissolved.

I took a sip of my drink, welcoming the burn it left down my throat.

My father stepped closer and pulled me into his arms. I stiffened. His grip tightened around me, and after a minute, I finally relaxed. "When you're ready, son, I'll explain everything. I love you so much, Riley. Trust me. Please." He paused. "Everything I did, I did it for you, son. I'm proud of the man you've become, and I'm sorry I hurt you. It has never been my intention."

His voice cracked. And a surge of emotions strangled me.

My father rarely spoke with his heart. But each time he did, his words sent a jolt to mine.

I hugged him back. Because even if I was all grown-up and stuff, I needed my father's love. Even when we didn't agree.

"Thanks. It means a lot. I'm sorry too, Dad," I said as I leaned back. I wiped the corners of my eyes with my thumb. "Can we get out of here? There's someone I want you to meet."

"Is it serious this time?"

"Yes. She's a keeper. I love her. It's still new, but I'm not letting her go."

———

After dinner, the four of us sat in the living room, drinks in hands. Hope slept in my mother's lap, snoring softly.

"Riley, I love this baby of yours. It's the cutest little thing I've seen in a long time. She's adorable. Now you'll make me long for grandchildren."

My jaw flexed. And my face must have turned a dark shade of red because Devon cocked her head in my direction and laughed.

"Mama. Come on. Now is not the time."

My mother shrugged. "I'm just saying. I've never pictured myself as a grandma before. But now I can see it."

I shook my head and huffed a long breath.

My mother switched her attention to Devon, patting her hand. "I didn't mean to put pressure on you, dear. I'm so happy you're here. It is about time Riley settled down with someone great. Again, I'm sorry if I overstepped. It's just that I've been wishing for him to find a woman who truly made him happy for so long. My Riley has a huge heart, but he's not always the best at letting other people in."

"*Mama,*" I warned.

She flicked her hand in the air.

"It's okay," Devon said. "I love hearing all about you. And I agree with Robin. Your heart is at the right place, Riley. I'm lucky I'm the woman you opened it to."

I lifted my ass from the chair I was sitting in and kissed her lips.

Hours without being able to touch her the way I craved felt like torture.

My father raised his tumbler. "Devon, this is your official welcome into the family." He moved to his feet and hugged her, dropping a kiss on her cheek. "And I couldn't agree more. You two look perfect for each other. Riley is lucky he found you."

A waterfall blurred my vision. *No, dad. She found me.* My father's words once again went straight to my heart, and I realized that, for the first time in my life, I had everything I ever wished for.

Hope made a yapping sound, and everyone burst out laughing, chasing away my emotional overload.

Maybe she agreed too.

Chapter 27

Devon

"My parents loved you," Riley said, holding my hand in his on the drive back. "Again, I'm sorry for my mother. She was out of line and a tad too assertive."

I grinned at Riley's perplexed expression, and I squeezed his upper arm.

"It's fine. She's your mom. She cares about you. I would give anything for my mother to be here and begging me for grandkids."

A tiny tremor shook my heart at the mention of my own mother.

"I'm sorry, Dev. I would have loved to meet her. I'm sure she was as amazing as you are. She still lives in you, though."

I closed my eyes to calm the emotions battling inside me. "I know. I'm sure she helped me escape that night. Gave me the courage to put a stop to the violence so I wouldn't end up like she did. For what it's worth, she would have loved you too. You remember I told you how much I loved fairy tales as a kid? Obsessed would be the correct term here. My mom would read me stories about knights in shining armor every night before bed and told me I looked like a princess." I paused, to settle the flutters firing inside me. "And you, Riley Burns, you made my little girl's wishes come true. You saved me. In more ways than you can imagine. You put pink and glitter in my gray existence. You showed me what true love is all about. And for that, I'll always be grateful."

We rode home in silence.

"Do you think you'll be ready to meet my friends next week?" my handsome man asked after he pulled the car into the garage. "Adam and Brooklyn will be in town on Friday night. They don't live around here, but every few weeks, we meet and catch up. This time they are flying here."

I looked at him. "I'd like that, but I won't intrude on your boys' night."

"You won't. You're in my life. I love you. I want my friends to get to know you."

Needy and missing the feel of his body, I moved to straddle him, playing with curls of his hair. A loud groan left Riley's mouth. I knew how he enjoyed my fingers massaging his scalp.

"You sure?"

We watched each other. The air thickened around us. My breast swelled at the heat searing through his gaze.

"Affirmative. And next month we're going to that fundraiser Carter and April are throwing to benefit their charity. It's their new project, and I'm sure it will be a success. Everything Carter touches turns to gold. Well… almost. I'll tell you stories some other time. Everyone I care about will be there. You'll fit right in. I know you will." Riley stole a kiss. "About Friday night, do you need to think about it?"

I shook my head. "Nah. I'll go wherever you go, Riley. Because I love you, and I trust you. Trusting someone was a big leap of faith for me, and you surpassed every expectation. I'd like you to meet my best friend too."

"The one from the rooftop bar who never showed up?"

"Yeah. The one."

Riley cradled my face with one hand. "Baby, I'm so sorry."

"It's okay. She's the only family I have left."

"Invite her over. If she's important to you, she's important to me too. And you have a family, Devon. Me. Hope. My parents. Soon my friends. You'll never be alone again. We're really a tight-knit circle, you'll see."

He unzipped my dress with steady fingers and peeled it down to my waist, his lips closing on my nipple after he pushed my bra cups down. "Now let's get you inside because the night isn't over yet, and I want to show you just how much I love you."

I laughed, grinding my hips against his, relishing the way my body caught fire when he fixed me with dark, sparkling eyes.

Hope woke up from her carrier and jumped between our connected bodies.

I kissed her furry head, tugging her to my heart. "I think someone is jealous," I said, laughing.

"Let's go on a short walk with her because I don't plan on sharing you tonight."

Riley zipped my dress back up, and we exited his car. He flushed; I aroused—or maybe it was the other way around.

He nipped my neck with his teeth, and I felt like I was about to dissolve right there on the garage floor.

"Riley," I moaned. My body ignited at all the right places. "Let's get this walk over with because I crave you. Like right about now."

He led the way after leashing our puppy, his hand strangling mine, the same desire taking over my body, mirrored in his irises.

Chapter 28
Riley

Wrapped in each other's arms, I combed Devon's curls with my fingers. My mouth found hers in the dark, and we lost ourselves in one of our *the world around us stops existing* kisses. The ones I'd never get enough of.

"I love you," I murmured against her mouth, positioning her against my heart, so she'd feel how much every particle in me loved her too.

She sank into my embrace and kissed my jaw. "I love you so much." Those three words reverberated through me and sent bolts of electricity straight through my heart. "Do you remember when you boosted that girl's self-confidence last year? The server? The one who dropped the wine all over you? Ohmygod, that was epic." Devon smiled at the memory, and it healed everything in me. "I was wrong when I said I fell in love with you when you washed my hair that night. It was when you gave that girl the pep talk."

"I wanted to go back home to change so bad that night. But I didn't want to be away from you. I would've spent the rest of the night in only my boxer briefs if it meant you would've been standing by my side. You made that much of an impression on me." I nuzzled the side of her face, teasing her earlobe with my teeth.

"When Robbie showed up, I thought I'd never see you again. I believed you'd think I was an escort or something."

My lips traveled down her throat, and massaged her breasts with my hands. Devon moaned in my ear.

"Question, though. How did you manage to get into the party? You never told me. The security was thorough." I curled a hand around her head and worked on her neck muscles. Devon rubbed herself against me, turning me into a puddle between her arms.

"My friend was seeing one of the waiters. He got us invites using fake names."

"For real?"

"She thought I deserved some harmless fun. I'd never done that before.. I mean sneaking into a private party. It was the first time. I just wanted to be someone else for a few hours."

I lowered my fingers between her thighs, rubbing her clit over the lace of her panties.

Devon's breathing quickened. And so did mine.

"I looked for you all night after you were gone. I even went through the guest list and surveillance videos."

She leaned back. "You did?"

"Yeah. I would've done just about anything for you back then."

"And now?" she asked, her tone teasing.

"Now you are my life, Devon." I claimed her lips, and she liquified when my tongue dived into her mouth.

"I know it's still new, but I'm where I'm supposed to be, Riley. I just know it."

"Move in with me."

Her warm chuckles resonated through the room. "I'm kind of already living here."

"Yeah, but let's make it official. Get your stuff and everything. Hope and I want you here full time. With us."

"I haven't been to my apartment since—" A chill moved along her spine, and it vibrated through me. I kissed her lips once more to ease the memory of that night.

"We can send people to pack your stuff. You don't have to go back there if you don't want to. Take some time to think about this, there's no rush."

"What if Robbie is released?"

"My lawyers will keep us updated. Don't worry about him anymore. He can't hurt you. Also, he has witnessed your strength the other night. It was pretty badass the way you knocked him down. That look on his face. You surprised the shit out of him. If I were him, I would think twice before coming anywhere near you ever again." I shifted to align my eyes with hers. "What's most important is that you're safe now, Dev."

"Have I told you already how much I love you?"

"Please tell me again because I think I'll never get used to it."

My lips tasted hers, and her hands traveled all over me. My entire body hummed under her touch.

Devon pushed back, just enough to stare at me, her eyes bright. "I love you, Riley Burns."

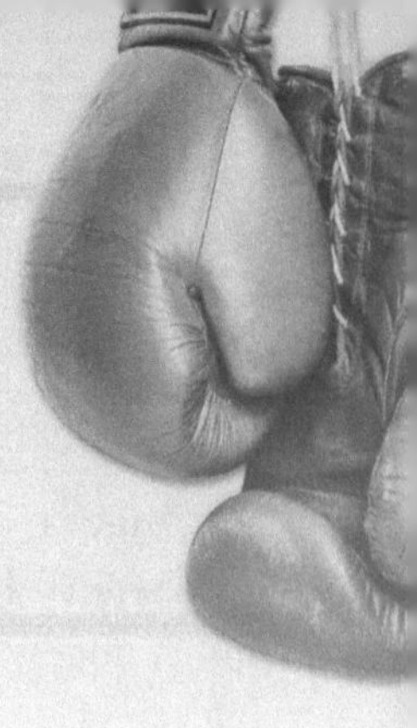

Epilogue
Devon

"Ohmygod, I can't believe you brought me to a Carter Hills concert," I said to my man. "I love the intimate set-up you guys created. It's much better than a show in a fifty-thousand-seat stadium."

"Yeah, I think it's pretty cool. When Carter decided to change the way he did concerts after April came along, I never thought it would be that successful. But again, he's Carter Hills. People would probably buy tickets to watch him flip burgers on a grill dressed in a panda suit."

"Wait until I suggest that April organize backyard shows. I'm sure, she'd like having a crowd watching them eat dinner dressed in animal costumes."

Riley tucked a strand of my hair behind my ear. "I'm glad you two became friends. I knew you'd get along fine. She reminds me of you. In many ways. You both fight hard for your happy ending. You deserve the best."

He kissed my forehead.

"Thanks. Don't downplay the role you played in mine, though, Riley Burns."

We kissed as the lights dimmed, the show about to start.

"Hey, I was wondering. Have you heard back from Aisha yet?" I asked in a whispered tone. Aisha Jones was his youngest artist, and she'd been having a hard time lately.

"Nah. I'll call her tomorrow morning and set up a meeting. She can't keep ignoring me whenever things get tough."

"You think she'll agree?"

He shrugged. "She has to. Don't worry. We'll talk about it later."

"I kinda like her," I said. "Even though we're about the same age, I can't help but feel protective of her."

"Yeah, I know you do. Don't worry, she'll be fine. I swear. When was the last time I didn't take care of my music family?"

I smiled at him. "Never. You're the most caring man I know. Carter, Aisha, Sam… They are lucky to have you in their lives watching their backs."

Carter walked onstage, and the crowd erupted in wolf-whistles and cheers.

It'd been ages since I went to a concert. When Riley asked if I'd prefer to watch from the side of the stage or the audience, I picked the latter to immerse myself in the full experience.

Carter crooned a few words to the overenthusiastic crowd and strummed the first chords of a song I didn't recognize. In the last three months I'd been with Riley, I'd listened to every song of every one of his artists because they mattered to him so they mattered to me too. And he mattered to me the most. I loved his music world. More than I ever expected to.

"This song is dedicated to my friend, Devon. Ry can't sing for shit, so he asked me to do him the honors. Devon, I know you're here tonight, and I want you to know you rock, girl. You're strong and fierce. And Ry is crazy about you. You are the best thing that has ever happened to him. Now he can't stop smiling like an idiot, but it suits him. It was about damn time. This song is truly special. So here it goes…"

I blinked a dozen times.

Did I hear him right?

Did Carter Hills just dedicate a song to me?

A song Riley wrote for me.

I blinked again.

My heart cartwheeled in my chest.

My palms turned moist.

Once I registered every word Carter spoke, I pivoted to face the man I loved.

"You did that?" I asked, my voice quivering with a storm of unleashed emotions.

He shrugged. "Already told you I can't sing. But I wanted you to have your own love song. Nobody's better than Carter Hills to deliver one."

"You wrote me a song?" I cupped my heart with both hands, begging it not to leave my chest cavity.

"I tried… Carter helped me. I'd never done this before. Please be indulgent. But know it comes from my heart. And that I love you—more with every single passing day."

I jumped into his arms, my feet not touching the floor when he lifted me higher, our bodies fusing together.

"Ohmygod, you wrote me a song. And you got Carter to sing it. Please tell me I'm not dreaming."

"Babe, it's happening. You deserve the best. Told you a thousand times. I love you, Devon."

My mouth crashed on his, letting it do the talking, unable to translate into words everything my heart felt.

> **Ooooh, you caught my eyes**
>   **that night**
> **Wearing a dress that made you**
>   **look divine**
> **Soon (too soon) you vanished**
>   **into the night**

A river streamed down my face. I couldn't believe our love story was now a song.

Our song.

Carter winked in our direction, and I formed a heart with my hands over my head. His smile doubled in size.

"You like it?" Riley asked, his arms locked around me.

"Are you kidding? It's the most thoughtful and amazing thing anyone has ever done for me. After giving me shelter the night I landed on their doorsteps covered in blood and with nowhere else to go."

Riley kissed my temple, and the melody of the song rocked the foundation of me.

> **Love, my heart wouldn't be full**
>   **without you**
> **Love, you are my dreams**
>   **come true**
> **Love, I'll love you with every-**
>   **thing that I am**
>
> **Ooooh, I love**
> **Ooooh, I love you forever**

I angled my upper body to kiss my wonderful man. "I love you forever too," I whispered against his lips.

"Great. Because that's just the beginning of our story."

The End

———

Meet Aisha Jones in Midnight Sparks
Grab your copy today

emmanuellesnow.com/products/midnight-sparks

Thank you for reading Riley and Devon's emotional and beautiful love story.

———

FREE bonus chapter
Want even more? Your bonus chapter awaits here
emmanuellesnow.com

Want more of Riley and Devon?

Read Fallen Legend: Sam Stevens's story
Read Midnight Spark: Aisha Jone's story

Curious about Carter Hills?
Read False Promises: Carter and April's story

WANT MORE EMOTIONAL LOVE STORIES?

WHICH COUPLE WILL YOU PICK NEXT?

False Promises

★★★★★ "The angst, the utter heartbreak, and protectiveness I felt for Carter during this book is unreal!"

★★★★★ "Emmanuelle Snow really knows how to tug at all of your emotions and does such a great job of bringing her characters to life!"

A gripping story of sizzling passion, lust, and the price of fame.
Start Carter Hills's story now

———

Sweet Agony

★★★★★ "If I could give more than 5 stars, I would."

★★★★★ "This is not a romance, it is a story about first love, first heartbreak and growing up."

A compelling tale of love, friendship, and self-discovery that will tug at your heartstrings.

Start Dahlia's story now

———

Cruel Destiny

★★★★★ "Wow. Just wow. If that could be my review, that is all I would write."

★★★★★ "Emmanuelle has done it yet again. She found a way to slip into my mind and heart with her words and the creation of characters you can't help but fall in love with."

★★★★★ "This book broke my heart in the first twenty five percent and sewed it back together."

A story of healing, second chances, and the risks of opening your heart to someone new. Can they trust each other with their hearts, or will their pasts keep them apart?

Read Nick and Dahlia's love story now

———

Wild Encounter

★★★★★ "This is by far one of the most well-written

book I've read this month. It is dynamic, intriguing, interesting, unafraid to go there and most of all touching."

★★★★★ "I personally wouldn't call this book JUST a romance novel because it's so much more. I 100% recommend it no doubt in mind."

A tale of passion and perseverance that will leave your heart racing and your spirit soaring.

Read Tucker and Addison's love story now

———

Last Hope

★★★★★ "This book was not only about the darkness but it was about pure love, hope, spice, family, and friendships on point with just the right amount without overpowering the storyline at all."

★★★★★ "Devon and Riley's story is a beautiful one with a lot of emotions. The subject matter is intense but it is handled very gently."

A tale of resilience and second chances in a world where love and danger intertwine.

Read Riley and Devon's love story now

———

Midnight Sparks

★★★★★ "The characters, the love, the humor, the steaminess, the emotions… it's everything I hoped and more."

★★★★★ "I think that is one Emmanuelle Snow's sexiest novels yet."

Welcome to the island where Holiday magic meets unexpected romance and a chance at a fresh start.

Read Gavin and Aisha's love story now

———

Fallen Legend

★★★★★ ""The love that grows, not only through tough angst but through unconditional moments had my heart. This is a spicy and riveting book"

★★★★★ "Emmanuelle Snow doesn't just tell a story, she creates an entire world."

A poignant and uplifting journey of hope, love, and the power of second chances.

Read Sam and Madison's love story now

———

Snowbound

★★★★★ "5 big stars from me for this amazing story. Absolutely loved it!"

★★★★★ "Emmanuelle Snow's stories are always full of angst, and Snowbound is no exception."

The intertwined lives of two strangers bound by fate in the midst of a snowstorm.

Read Anderson and Abigail's love story now

———

All available at emmanuellesnow.com

ACKNOWLEDGMENTS

Oh wow, I can't believe Riley and Devon's story is finally here. This book began as a short story last year, but it didn't feel complete, so I decided to build it into a full-length novel.

Devon and Riley's journey to love is sprinkled with moments of hurt and darkness I wish no human being would have to go through.

But since I'm dedicated to writing realistic and relatable stories, this delicate topic had to be depicted sensitively, and I hope you agree I did it with lots of love and hope, even through the dark times.

Because behind every shadow, there's a light waiting to shine on its own, to regain the place it deserves in this life.

Not all love stories are rainbow and unicorn because hey, that's how life works. But with each challenge comes a dose of hope that things will work out in the end. And no matter what, I'm a firm believer we must keep that little flame alive in our hearts when everything is crumbling around us because that's the hope that keeps us going.

If you have ever gone through an abusive relationship or hard times, I'm sending you a virtual hug. And if things are tough, please remember, as Devon's mom would say, the sun always comes out after the storm.

I want to thank all the people who've supported me through the writing of this book. My little Snow squad, I love you and will fight for you forever. My husband, who believes in me through the good and bad times. I love you.

Shalini, who's not only my books' fairy godmother, but my friend. Your heart is at the right place, and you push me to be a better author and also a better person every day. Thank you for everything.

My readers, you make this journey a meaningful one. I think everyone knows by now I'm a crier for everything emotional and beautiful. All your good words, messages, reviews go straight to my heart.

My ARC team and the reviewers (Bloggers, Bookstagrammers, Tik-Tokers, YouTubers, etc.) who give my books a chance, it is the most amazing feeling when you say YES. I'm so grateful to have all of you in my corner. Sincerely.

As my editor and I would say, this is a wrap!

Cheers!

ABOUT THE AUTHOR

Soulfully Beautiful Love Stories

USA Today Bestselling Author Emmanuelle Snow is an author of contemporary YA and women's fiction love stories, who gives life to strong characters who'll fight with all they have to reach their life goals and find their own happiness. She loves her characters to be relatable and realistic.

Emmanuelle is in love with love. Especially complicated, deep, and passionate feelings that make a relationship extraordinary and complex all at the same time.

In her spare time, when she's not writing or reading, she likes to go on road trips—with her four kids and her own soulmate—watch movies, paint, or do some DIY, always with a cup of green tea in her hand and listening to country music.

She splits her time between beautiful Canada and the small US towns she adores.

Find all of Emmanuelle's books here:
emmanuellesnow.com

———

Want to connect with Emmanuelle online?

YOU CAN FIND HER HERE:

Website

Author's bookstore and merch store

Snow's VIP newsletter

emmanuellesnow.com

Readers' VIP group Snow's Soulmates

facebook.com/groups/snowvip

amazon.com/author/emmanuellesnow

goodreads.com/emmanuellesnow

bookbub.com/authors/emmanuelle-snow

facebook.com/esnowauthor

instagram.com/snowemmanuelle

x.com/snowemmanuelle

pinterest.com/snowemmanuelle

tiktok.com/@snowemmanuelle

ALSO BY THE AUTHOR

CARTER HILLS BAND UNIVERSE

(suggested reading order)

Carter Hills Band series

False Promises

Heart Song Duet

Blindsided

Forevermore

Whiskey Melody series

Sweet Agony

Second Tear Duet

Cruel Destiny

Beautiful Salvation

Breathless Duet

Wild Encounter

Brittle Scars

Upon A Star Series

Last Hope

Midnight Sparks

Love Song For Two Series

EMMANUELLE

SNOW

MIDNIGHT SPARKS

AISHA

I threw in my black heels and zipped up my suitcase. I was so done. Nothing could keep me here—not even the holidays, especially the ones at the end of the year. I hated everything about Christmas. The cheer. The smiles from strangers. The camaraderie. And don't get me started on those cookies and carols. God, those were the worst. Whoever invented the holiday traditions must have done it as a sick joke. And now the entire freaking world was obsessed with them. Well done, champ.

With one last glance around my bedroom, I made sure I had everything I needed for this trip. Two weeks on an island in the middle of the Caribbean Sea, with an open bar and palm trees. I knew I had packed the right outfits.

Little black dress that made my legs look longer. *Check.*

Sparkling red dress that gave my boobs all the attention they deserved. *Check.*

Sunblock, shades, and hat. *Check. Check. And check.*

Oh yes, the tiny white string bikini I could flaunt my curves in. *Check too.*

My phone buzzed. Of course, it was my manager. I

rolled my eyes because I didn't even have to look to know what the message said.

RILEY

Did you change your mind about that holiday special in Times Square?

Laughter rose in my chest and burst free, echoing louder than it should have. As if Riley didn't know better. I didn't do Christmas shows. Never. He knew it. But that didn't stop him from trying to convince me.

Every single year.

ME

Forget it. And Carter or whoever else you want me to sing a duet with. No special appearance. Me + island = perfect vacation. Talk to you next year, Ry.

RILEY

If you change your mind, kiddo, you know where to find me.

ME

Sorry. Not happening.

RILEY

Fine. Didn't hurt to try. Maybe someday you'll actually say yes to me. Keeping my fingers crossed.

ME

In your dreams. But I love you for looking out for me. Have a blast with Santa and his bunch of stupid elves.

In the entryway, I slid my phone into the back pocket of my jeans, and adjusting my lacy black top, I perused my image in the mirror, debating whether to let my hair loose or not. This morning, I woke up early to straighten my black curls. It took me over an hour to get them to behave. I gathered my hair into a ponytail, held it for a second, then let it fall. Hair down it was. With one sweep, I colored my lips in ruby red—*Passion red*, they called it—suiting my dark complexion perfectly, and applied a thick coat of mascara to the lashes framing my dark kohl-lined eyes. From a hook behind the door, I grabbed my jacket, the one matching my lipstick, and got the hell out of my house before someone else tried to change my mind.

Last year, I went to Fiji for the holidays. The year before, I traveled to the wildest parts of Australia. I chose my destinations with a single goal in mind: anywhere I could fade from sight for two weeks. This year, I had chosen Playa De La Isla Azul, a small island in the Caribbean Sea, with a population of less than two thousand and a handful of resorts. It was so small that planes only landed there once or twice a week. Someone on my last tour recommended it, and I had decided to give it a try. It was exactly the kind of place where someone could disappear for a while.

The cab driver climbed out of the car to grab my suitcase and stuffed it in the trunk. With careful steps, I tried not to get too much snow into my shoes. Sure, golden heels weren't the most convenient to walk in Tennessee at this time of the year, but they made me feel powerful. And sexy. So be damned the frost bites. My toes could suffer until we reached the airport.

The cab pulled away. Out the back window, my house grew smaller, its roof and front yard dusted with a thin layer of snow. I let out a long, slow sigh. My shoulders relaxed with each mile away as I sank into the seat, the tension in my upper back dissolving and excitement unfurling in the pit of my stomach. Yes, I was long overdue for a vacation, and more than ready to let the good times roll.

The driver turned the radio on, and a Christmas song I knew too well drifted through the air, filling the space around me.

With a roll of my eyes and doing my best to avoid grimacing, I pleaded to the driver, "I'll give you an extra tip—fifty bucks—if you turn that damn thing off right now."

Our gazes met in the rearview mirror.

"You serious?"

"Dead serious." I flashed him a grin, just for good measure.

"Fine. The lady wins," he agreed with a wink. I sighed. I couldn't wait to be out of here. He droned on, "You're not a fan of the holidays as I can see. I thought singers like you, the ones singing love songs for a living, fancied all things romantic. Forget Valentine's Day, Christmas is the real deal. The most romantic time of the year."

"Well, people like me don't all enjoy this shit. It's over-rated. Commercial. Full of clichés. No, thanks. I'll choose palm trees over candy canes any day."

"You'd be surprised how the holidays can win you over."

I snorted. "Don't think so."

With earbuds in, I slumped in my seat, watching the Nashville skyline through the window as it disappeared, the more we neared the airport.

———

Read Aisha Jones's story,
read Midnight Sparks now

emmanuellesnow.com/products/midnight-sparks

Author's bookstore at emmanuellesnows.com

*"I think that is one Emmanuelle Snow's
sexiest novels yet." (Goodreads)*

*"This story warmed my heart, and I was so
engrossed in the story I never wanted
to put it down." (Goodreads)*

Midnight Sparks is book two in the
Love Song For Two series.

Read **Midnight Sparks** now

HOPE